DEAD &
BURIED

A gripping crime thriller full of twists

HELEN H. DURRANT

D1440494

Published 2016 by Joffe Books, London.

www.joffebooks.com

ISBN-13: 978-1-911021-64-3

Prologue

It is sometime in the late 1960s. A teenage boy is hammering on the door of a cottage. On the steps sits a girl, obviously in pain, clutching at her stomach . . .

"Help her! She's not right! Open up now or I'll knock the bloody door down!"

"Granny Slater said we should give her a while." The girl's friend held a bottle of water to her lips. "It'll pass. I'm sure it's just what happens."

"Bollocks! She's losing far too much blood."

The friend looked down: he was right. Blood seeped down the steps and the girl was writhing in agony.

"If she doesn't come out now and do something, I'll blow her bloody head off."

The friend looked up and gasped. "Vinny! Where did you get that?" She knew Vinny was a hard nut. She'd warned the girl often enough. But a gun!

"This . . ." he waved the revolver in front of her face. "It's my faithful little friend. I never leave home without it these days. Life's too dangerous."

Granny Slater opened a bedroom window and shouted down. "Get her out of here! I've done my bit. She'll be alright, just give her time."

"You've fucking butchered her, you cow."

The girl whimpered and then keeled over. Vinny knelt down beside her. "Her breathing's gone funny."

"We need to get a doctor." The friend was frantic. This wasn't supposed to happen. Plenty of other girls had come up here to see Granny Slater and everything had been fine. But now. Something had gone wrong. "She could die, Vinny, and this is against the law. We'll get into trouble."

"That's why we can't get no doctor up here. He'd just call the police."

"We've got to do something. We can't just leave her like this."

"Hey! Bitch! Do you want that?" Vinny yelled up at the window. "Do you want me to call a doctor and have you put away?"

The door opened and Granny Slater looked at the girl. "She's had a bad reaction, that's all."

But her friend knew the girl was done for. The lifeblood was pouring out of her and they couldn't make it stop.

"Bring her in," the old woman said.

Vinny carefully gathered the girl in his arms. She screamed in pain. Her friend winced. This had been a bad idea. They shouldn't have come. She should have told her mother the truth and had the baby.

Vinny carried the girl into the kitchen. "You're one evil witch!" he hissed at the woman. "Where do I put her?"

Granny Slater pointed to the kitchen table.

Vinny laid her down on top of a dark red stain in the open grain of the pine top. There was still a pool of blood on the stone-flagged floor. The friend was shaking. The kitchen made her think of the butcher's shop in Leesdon.

Granny Slater went to the sideboard and took out a leather-bound notebook. A small child was standing in the shadows, watching. "Get to your room," bawled the woman. "Sharpish, or you'll get a clout round the ear."

"You're wasting time! Get on with it." Vinny was screaming now.

"I have to get rid of the kid," she screeched back. "She can't see this. You said three months gone?"

The friend nodded.

Vinny was still holding the gun.

"Should have been easy." She put the book away.

"Just sort her out!" Vinny jabbed the weapon into her ribs.

"I'll do what I can."

But there was a look of fear in the woman's eyes. The friend saw it and knew. The cottage suddenly seemed deathly quiet and cold. The girl on the table wasn't walking out of here tonight. She'd be lucky to make it through the next hour.

"If she dies, then so do you." Vinny's voice was icy.

The friend shrieked at them. "We have to get help!"

Vinny waved the gun. "Well?"

"She's beyond help." The woman looked at the body on the table, now lifeless.

"No, Vinny!" The friend made a dive for the hand holding the gun. "Don't do this. You mustn't."

The two struggled in the semi-gloom. The old woman watched, rooted to the spot in fear. Then, amid the screams and raised voices, a single shot rang out.

Chapter 1

Now — Tuesday

She lay flat on her back on the grass, her arms neatly folded over her chest. Her skin was the colour of milk. Her eyes were wide open, staring sightlessly at the sun. Half a dozen bluebottles hovered over the body. Others had already settled on the blood seeping through her clothing.

"How long?" DI Tom Calladine asked the pathologist.

"A few hours. Rigor is still present. Plus it rained last night and she isn't wet."

"Rocco!" shouted Calladine. "Have a look for wheel marks on that grass track down there. She got up here somehow."

"There's nothing!"

They were standing on a hillside above Leesdon. DI Tom Calladine, DC Simon Rockliffe, a forensic team from the Duggan and Bob Bower, the pathologist standing in for Natasha Barrington. Notably absent was Calladine's

4

partner, Sergeant Ruth Bayliss. Ruth was still on maternity leave after the birth of her son.

"Brought here and then killed?" Calladine asked Doctor Bower. "If not, whoever did this must have carried her."

"Why do you say that?" the pathologist asked.

"Look at her shoes. There would be scuff marks on them if she'd had to walk up the hill."

The pathologist removed one of the shoes. "Dirt on the soles of her feet," he said. "Looks like she took them off."

"And then the killer put them on again? Odd thing to do."

"It is murder then, sir?" asked a uniformed officer.

"I doubt she shot herself in the back, Constable. Anyone recognise her?" Calladine looked round.

Rocco shook his head.

"I think she's Ricky Blackwell's mum," the uniform chipped in. "They live in Leesdon, on the Hobfield."

"Who found her?"

"A walker, sir. He's been taken back to the station to make a statement."

"Anyone found her belongings? Bag? Phone?"

More head shaking.

"How old would you say she was?" Calladine asked the pathologist.

"Early fifties. Difficult to tell though, she's looked after herself."

Unusual for someone from the Hobfield estate. The place was a sinkhole containing all of Leesdon's troublemakers and no-hopers. It could hardly be called a beacon of clean, healthy living. But this woman was different. Her clothes for a start. They looked expensive. Not that Calladine was any expert. Her make-up was perfect. Her lipstick looked as if she'd just applied it. Her dark hair was cut short and looked freshly combed.

"Deliberately laid out like this — what do you think?" Calladine stood up.

"Well, she's not been left as she fell, that's for sure. Both her legs are broken. From the bruising, I'd say something had hit her in the knees, full on." Bower felt one of them with his gloved hand. "The kneecap feels as if it's completely smashed. Not content with that, they hit her on the back of the head." He looked up. "Quite a significant injury. She'd have fallen forward. There are no defence injuries either." He raised a manicured hand.

"Fallen onto her front?"

"I'd say so. There is extensive bruising to her face."

"Disabled first, then shot?"

"Possibly. I'll be certain when the PM's done. But it's probable that the head wound alone would have killed her within a short time."

"Killed here, then," Calladine said.

"More than likely. But like you say, not dressed for walking. Tight skirt, high heels. She looks like she was on her way out somewhere."

Calladine turned to the PC. "What do we know about the Blackwell family?"

"Son tries to be a bit of a tearaway. Influenced by others, that's his trouble."

Calladine sighed. Kids. He looked around him. This was not a day you'd choose to die, nor was this the place. The scenery and the weather were glorious — rare for this part of the world. The hills were bathed in summer sunshine, and the sky was a cloudless blue. "We'll get a positive identification. In the meantime I'll let you get on with it."

"Doctor Barrington said it would be quiet," Doctor Bower complained. "She's only been away three days and we've had two fatal road accidents already. Now this."

"When's she back?"

"A few days, apparently."

Calladine looked at the forensic team working on the scene. No Julian. The team were now headed up by a woman — forensic scientist Doctor Roxy Atkins.

"There are a whole lot of tracks going off up that way." Roxy pushed back the hood of her coverall. "No tyre tracks, just footprints. Where does it go?"

"Clough Bottom, a small hamlet and local beauty spot. A magnet for ramblers," Calladine told her. "Like all the hills around here. Over there, that's Wharmton. The one with the jagged-looking tops behind you is Indian's Head."

She smiled. "Strange names."

"Strange place," he said.

"We'll take a look at the tracks, but being so many I can't promise anything."

Calladine gestured to DC Simon Rockliffe, known to his workmates as Rocco. "We'll head back."

* * *

The woman strode into the auction room and took a seat at the front. She was tall with long, dark hair to her shoulders and wore expensive designer clothing. Every pair of eyes bar Imogen Goode's studied her with silent curiosity. Then the whispering started. She was quite striking and she wasn't local. So who was she?

Imogen nudged her companion. "Wind your neck in." She slapped Julian Batho's arm. "She's far too old for you, and don't forget why we're here. It's next up. It should go for a song, it's in such a bad state."

"No one has lived in it for at least four decades. Plus it looks like the local kids have tried to demolish it. The walls for example — you saw the state they're in. They've kicked the plaster off most of them."

Imogen slapped him again. "How about a bit of enthusiasm?"

"There are plenty of nice houses in town."

Same old argument.

"Clough Cottage is the back of beyond," he continued. "A couple of miles out of Leesdon town. Nearest neighbour half a mile away up that hill there," he pointed. "What happens up there when it snows?"

"You use a four-wheel drive, Julian. Stop being difficult."

Detective Constable Imogen Goode and Professor Julian Batho from the Duggan Centre had been an item for several months now. Neither of them was in any doubt that this was the real thing, so they had decided to buy a property together. Since then they'd bickered almost nonstop. An old cottage off the Huddersfield Road above Leesdon had come up for auction. It had been empty for years. A local builder had described it as a money pit, but that hadn't put Imogen off. She liked the idea of being away from people. Apart from that, when it was renovated the cottage would be worth real money. But Julian Batho wasn't so sure. He was no DIY expert.

Imogen heard male voices coming from the back of the room and turned to look. "What's he doing here?"

Julian recognised Jacob Naden. "He's a local farmer," he said.

"Yes I know that." Imogen watched a middle-aged man walk to the front of the room, accompanied by a boy who was obviously his son. "He could be a serious contender," she whispered. "He owns Clough Farm, that neighbour you were talking about, up on the tops above the cottage."

The auctioneer called for silence. Clough Cottage was next up.

"Go on," she urged, tucking a lock of long blonde hair behind her ear. "Get it bought."

Julian raised his card. He went straight in on the opening bid. There was silence. Imogen waited, hardly daring to breath. If no one else was interested, it was seconds away from being theirs.

Then all hell let loose. Bids came from every corner of the room.

"Why? I don't understand. Most of the folk here don't look as if they've got two halfpennies to rub together," said Julian.

"You shouldn't take the people round here at face value, Julian. Folk don't broadcast their wealth."

Above the din of the bidding, a voice shouted out.

"I'll double it!"

Silence fell and all eyes swung towards the unknown woman. She looked back at Imogen and Julian.

"It's still not much. Bid again," Imogen hissed, glaring daggers at the woman. She had an American accent. Not strong, it was the sort you'd pick up from living there for a few years.

Jacob Naden was scowling. "Not so fast, lady. That's not how it's done." He upped the bid by twenty thousand.

Julian put a consoling arm around Imogen's waist. "It's way out of our league now. That pair will fight it out to the death."

He was right. Imogen was disappointed but also intrigued. The cottage was only a stone's throw from Naden's farm, so she could understand his interest. But she had no idea who the woman was and why she wanted the cottage. The entire room was watching as she and Naden stared each other down.

"This is highly irregular," said the auctioneer, his face florid, gavel in hand.

There was more muttering around the room. Then the woman's mobile rang. "Give me a moment," she mouthed to the auctioneer and hurried to the back of the room.

The auctioneer leaned forward. "Mr Batho? Do you want to make a higher offer?"

"It's pointless," Julian whispered to Imogen. He turned to the auctioneer. "Let them fight it out. We can't outbid either of them."

The auctioneer looked up to call the woman back but she had gone. Jacob Naden clapped his son on the back. The cottage was theirs.

* * *

Imogen looked up from her computer screen. "Ricky Blackwell is on the system, sir. Petty theft from local shops, nothing serious, and no dealing. His mother's name is Emily."

"Address?"

"Second floor, Heron House. Number twelve."

"Well, we need to confirm if this is Ricky's mother or not. Rocco — we'll get round there."

"How did it go this morning?" Rocco asked Imogen before they left.

"It didn't. We were outbid — quite dramatically too. The place is practically derelict but folk were falling over themselves to buy it."

"Who got it in the end?"

"The Nadens got it. But it was tough going. Some woman was fighting Jacob Naden tooth and nail."

"You'll find something," Calladine assured her. "Why not speak to Zoe's partner, Jo. She's an estate agent. I'm sure she'll help."

"Actually that's not a bad idea."

Zoe was Calladine's daughter. She was a solicitor and her partner, Jo Brandon, was an estate agent. Between the two of them they more or less had the Leesdon property market sewn up.

As they left, Calladine heard Imogen on the phone to Julian. She was suggesting exactly that.

"Wonder what she did to end up dead, sir," Rocco said to Calladine.

"Crossed some scroat — easy to do when you live where she did."

"She didn't look the type to live on the Hobfield. She looked too classy."

"Classy clothes — doesn't mean she was a classy woman. She probably had some money to spare, that's all. And money to spare can be a dangerous thing on that estate."

"DI Calladine!" Rhona Birch called out as they passed her office door.

He rolled his eyes. "Give me a minute, Rocco. You go sort the car."

Calladine poked his head through the half-open door. "Yes, ma'am?"

"Come in. Take a seat. I've had Superintendent McCabe on from Daneside."

"What have we done to interest him?"

"We have a body, as well you know. He is heading up the new Major Incident Team, so it's his job to be interested."

"I thought they'd decided to leave us out. I read the memo. It said the team would only involve Oldston, Daneside and parts of East Manchester."

"That might be the case eventually, but for now they're still making up their minds." She paused for a moment, a frown creasing her masculine features "I have to say their interest has aroused my curiosity. We've had incidents recently that they have completely ignored. So what could be different about this one?"

"Perhaps they're short of something to do."

Rhona Birch didn't look amused.

"Keep your eyes and ears open, Inspector, and keep me informed." The look she gave him could freeze the soul. "And be warned. If they do send someone, it'll be a DCI."

In that case he'd keep his fingers crossed that it wasn't the newly promoted DCI Greco.

Chapter 2

The punch landed hard. The young man fell back onto the concrete floor, banging his head. He ran a tentative hand over his face — blood. The bastard had bust his nose.

"You let us down," Kayne Archer said, kicking his leg. "You were asked to do a simple job. You got it wrong and that's no good to me. Get stuff wrong again and I'll take you apart."

"I can't do it. I'd be no good at it," Ricky said. He shuffled away, on his backside.

"You'll be fine. You need to toughen up."

"I'm not like you. I can't get away when I want to."

"In that case you'd better make some changes. I want you on the team. Refuse again and you'll suffer."

"No," Ricky said, holding the bottom of his T-shirt against his nose. "I don't want any part of it." Ricky was terrified. He'd never faced up to Archer and his crew before. They could do him some serious harm. He decided to chance it. "Mr Costello wouldn't like it." He'd heard his mother whispering to her sister about someone called Costello. He'd no idea who he was, only that he was trouble. But he had no other defence against this lot. There were three of them — Mick Garrett and Wayne

12

Davey, but it was Archer who was baying for blood. Ricky's eyes flitted over their faces. Archer wanted to lamp him one. He had his fist ready, poised behind his head.

"You're playing a dangerous game." Archer's arm came down and he flexed his fingers. He poked Blackwell's chest instead of caving his skull in.

That had been close. Ricky Blackwell felt sick.

"Don't take Costello's name in vain," warned Archer. "You need to be careful. You never know who's listening."

It had worked, though. Archer gave him a long, hard look, grunted an expletive and took off with the two others behind him.

Ricky Blackwell struggled to his feet. He felt dizzy. His head hurt and blood from his nose had stained his clothes. But he'd got off lightly. Whoever Costello was, Ricky owed him.

Archer and his cronies had collared him in an alleyway across the square from Heron House where he lived. Like most people his age on the Hobfield, they didn't like him.

Ricky tried to keep his head down. It was a matter of self-preservation. He was a natural target for any would-be villain who fancied his chances. He was twenty-two years old but looked at least five years younger. He was small, thin and pale and had a reputation as a mummy's boy.

Despite treating him as some sort of joke, Kayne Archer was trying to recruit him. He wanted him to run drugs — become a delivery boy. The idea was that Archer would give him the drugs and then Ricky would ride round the estate on his bike, delivering and collecting the money. Ricky would get a cut. But it wouldn't be long before Archer was feeding him drugs too. Then the money would stop and payment would be made in his drug of choice. Ricky's mother had warned him. She'd forbidden him to have anything to do with the likes of Archer. But it wasn't easy.

Ricky brushed himself down. He'd straighten himself out when he got to work. He had been promised a shift at the café on Leesdon High Street. With a bit of luck he could sponge the blood from his clothes. He didn't want his mother worrying. Mind you, the worrying worked both ways. She'd gone out early this morning, saying she'd be gone all day. He wasn't daft. He knew she was seeing someone and she didn't want him finding out.

* * *

"What d'you reckon that lot have been up to?" Calladine had spotted the knot of young men emerging from the alleyway.

"The tall one's Kayne Archer, sir — right tearaway. Rumour has it he's dealing dope on the estate, but we don't know who for."

"Get uniform to keep an eye out. The first hint that he is — drag him in. Fallon's death has left a huge gap. All the villains in Greater Manchester must be falling over themselves to fill it. It's only a matter of time before one of them becomes head man around here. Who are the other two?"

"Mick Garrett — another right hothead, and Wayne Davey. Davey wouldn't be trouble on his own but put him with that pair and anything's possible."

"So they're the next generation of trouble we've to contend with."

"Who do you reckon is ahead — for the post of top dog, sir? One of them?"

"It could be anyone. The Manchester villains will all be in the running."

"Anyone in mind?"

"No, Rocco, but that doesn't stop me from having a bad feeling. Sooner or later someone will show their hand. This estate is literally going begging."

"Should we stop them, sir? Have a word?"

"No, Rocco, leave them for now. It's not the right time."

The two detectives made their way up to the second floor of the tower block. Number twelve looked okay. Like the body at the scene, it looked well kept. There were decent curtains at the windows and the paintwork was fresh and clean. Whoever Emily Blackwell had been, she'd had her standards.

Rocco knocked and they waited.

"No one in, sir,"

"We could do with finding him." Calladine looked up and down the deck. "I'll try next door."

A woman answered. Calladine showed her his badge.

"We're looking for Ricky Blackwell. Do you have any idea where we can find him?"

"Ricky? He went out earlier. He might have gone to work or the job centre."

"Where does he work? It's important we speak to him."

"He gets the odd hour at the café on the High Street. He might be there. Is Ricky in trouble?"

"No."

"So what do you want him for? His mum shouldn't be long."

"Do you know Ricky's mum well?" Calladine asked.

"She's my sister."

* * *

"We now have a positive identification," Calladine told the team. "The woman killed on the hillside was Emily Blackwell. Rocco and I went to her flat on the Hobfield looking for the son, Ricky, but we couldn't find him. We'll go back shortly. His aunt, Emily's sister, is going to collect him from work. She agreed to do the identification and I've just come from taking her to the Duggan. She confirmed the body is that of her Emily and gave me a current photo." He pinned it to the incident board.

15

Imogen looked up from her usual place behind her computer. "I've already started some background searches. Emily is divorced. We looked at her bank account and she didn't have a fortune coming in. Oldston Council paid her salary each month so I presume she worked for them. But there is something else."

"Go on," Calladine prompted.

"A small amount of money was paid in each month. It has being going on for years — a company called 'Jet Holdings.'"

"Do we know who they are?"

"No. Tracing them is proving difficult and it shouldn't be. I'll get on to the bank and see what they know."

"Does her bank account say who she paid her mobile phone bill to?"

Imogen nodded.

"Get on to the service provider for a list of calls and texts. It's probably switched off now or run out of battery, but make sure."

"Emily was dressed up," he continued. "She looked as if she was going somewhere — make-up, high heels." Calladine was pacing up and down. "We need to know where, who with and how she got to where she was found. Was she meeting a man, for instance?"

"Odd if she was," Rocco chipped in. "Folk don't usually arrange a date halfway up a hill."

"There was the auction today, sir," Imogen reminded him.

"Yes but that took place in the town. Presumably all the viewing had been done."

"The Nadens bought Clough Cottage but there would have been other viewings. There was a woman for example. We didn't know her and she was a bit last minute. She was dead keen to buy the place. She looked the part too. You know, plenty of money behind her. Next thing, she gets a phone call and does one. She sounded

American. She may well have looked at the cottage earlier or last night and seen something."

Imogen had a point. "Ring the auctioneers and check it out. See if they know who the woman was."

"We need to find her son, sir," Rocco volunteered. "He may know who those payments came from and where Emily was going."

"Inspector!" DCI Birch came into the office and nodded at the team. "I've had McCabe on the phone again. He does want a member of his new team in on this but he won't say why. He says it's because of the murder but I'm not sure I believe him."

"What other reason could there be, ma'am?"

"It could be anything. I know him of old. He's hiding something."

"Does he have a particular DCI in mind?"

"Yes, he does."

"In that case let's hope we can entertain him," Calladine said lightly. "So far it's a fairly straightforward murder — if murder can ever be described as straightforward." He tried a smile. "So — go on. Who do we get?"

The entire team were aware that Calladine didn't want to work with Stephen Greco again. They waited with bated breath for Birch to reply.

"They are sending us someone new, a DCI King."

There were sighs of relief.

"So we're to have a spy in the camp." Calladine was trying to keep it light for the team. "That's a new one. Perhaps the real reason is to check on our performance."

"She, Calladine. DCI King is a woman. And no, I don't think that's it."

"Every cloud . . ." but he pulled a face. "You never know, she might let us in on whatever's going on."

"She might have to. DCI King won't get far working alone."

So Birch wasn't thrilled either. She left the room.

"As if we didn't have enough to think about," Rocco said.

Calladine looked at the incident board. It was almost empty. "Come on then. Let's see if we can get a bit more information up there before this woman turns up. All we have so far is a name, Emily Blackwell, and a location."

"Sir, it was a Mrs Mallon who bid on the cottage," Imogen interrupted.

"Do we know anything about her?"

"No, but she must have some money behind her. Before she got that phone call she'd doubled the existing bid — ours. She was determined to get the place."

"Get some background on her too," Calladine told Imogen.

Chapter 3

"This place doesn't change much, does it, sir?"

"No, Rocco."

"To their credit the council does try. Look at the wall over there. At some time the parks department has put flowers in those planters."

"Waste of time and money. The little thugs have kicked them to shreds.

"You have to wonder why. There's just no sense in such mindless vandalism."

The two were parked at the edge of the Hobfield. They were watching a group of youngsters on push bikes. They had gathered in a circle and an older teenager was speaking to them.

"Bet that's nothing to do with cycling proficiency," Rocco joked.

"Who is that, the one in the middle?"

"Wayne Davey. He's one of Kayne Archer's mates. We saw them earlier."

"Is he local?"

"Very much so — born and raised here."

"How old?"

"He must be about nineteen or twenty. He's never had a job as far as I know. He allegedly lives with his mother. But intel from the uniform who keeps an eye out says he's squatting with some others in an empty flat in Egret House." He nodded towards a tower block.

"They are up to something. Let's take a look," said Calladine.

They got out of the car and walked across the barren concrete square. Davey spotted them and grinned cheekily.

"Go on, lads, get lost. The pigs are here," he said as the detectives approached. The pack sped off in different directions leaving him standing alone.

"Quite a fan club you've got," said Calladine.

"Just giving them a little friendly advice. Kids on here have to know the rules."

"Where's your mate — Archer?" Calladine asked.

"How should I know?"

"You're rarely apart these days. But you should be careful. Archer and Garrett are a bad lot. My advice is to keep away."

"You don't frighten me," said Wayne. "I've done nowt and neither's Kayne, so you can get lost."

"You need to learn some manners," Calladine told him.

The lad laughed, cleared his throat and spat onto the ground.

"What rubbish were you feeding that crew?"

"Telling them like it is, wasn't I? They want something, they come to us."

He'd never dare be so full of it back in the Fallon era, thought Calladine.

"Got a new big man on the block, have you?"

The lad laughed. "Oh yeah, the biggest. You need to watch your step, copper."

Behind them a huge black limo with dark tinted windows pulled silently onto the spare land in front of Heron House. Davey's face fell.

"I've got to go." He pulled up his hood and hunched over, reducing his six feet by several inches. He looked fearful. "You're wasting your time harassing me. I don't talk to coppers."

As if a switch had flicked, Davey had gone from being a cocky bugger to a frightened little boy. He was edgy and his eyes flitted around him.

"Afraid someone will see us together, son?" Calladine turned to look at the limo. "You need to learn how to relax. All that tension isn't good for you."

Davey was mumbling now. "I need to go. I can't tell you anything."

"Never said you could, lad. Just thought we'd say hello." Calladine smiled and clapped Davey affably on the shoulder. He and Rocco walked towards Heron House.

"Get the number of that car?" he asked Rocco.

"Yes, sir."

"Ring it in to Imogen and get her to find out who owns it. I could be wrong, but I reckon it was someone taking a long, hard look."

"At Davey, sir?"

"Yes. Him and the Hobfield. Weighing up the competition and what the estate has to offer."

By the time they reached the second floor, Calladine was panting.

"You should consider doing more exercise, sir," said Rocco.

"Cheeky sod. This is the second time today I've climbed these damned steps, I'll have you know. You do know how old I am?"

"Do no harm though, would it? Age is no barrier to fitness. There's a new gym in Leesdon, down by the swimming pool."

"Any good?"

"They've got all the gear and some great offers."

"I'll think about it."

They knocked at the door of Emily Blackwell's sister.

"He's very upset, Inspector," Enid Mason told him. "And I'm not too clever myself after that visit to the morgue. Seeing Emily like that — her death. It's given us both a shock."

"We won't stay long but we would like to speak to him. It's important that we know as much about Emily's background as we can."

"I can tell you anything you want to know. She only lived next door. We saw each other every day."

"It's okay, Auntie. I can do this."

Ricky Blackwell emerged from a bedroom. He stood in front of them in loose tracksuit bottoms and a T-shirt. He had a cut on his lip and one eye was bruised.

"You've taken quite a pasting, son," said Calladine, moving closer to look. "Who'd you upset?"

Ricky shrugged. "It's nowt, honest. A run-in earlier with some idiots. They pick on everybody. Today it was my turn."

"Those idiots wouldn't be Archer and his chums, would they?"

Ricky Blackwell shook his head but didn't answer.

"I need to ask you about your mother, son," Calladine said kindly.

"Go through and sit down," Enid offered. "I'll make some tea."

The two detectives followed Ricky through to the sitting room. The place was clean and nicely furnished. Not what they were used to seeing on the Hobfield.

"You're staying with your auntie then, Ricky?"

"Yeah. I won't be able to keep the flat on. The rent's too much."

"Do you know where your mum was going today?" Calladine asked.

He shook his head. "Work, I thought."

"Do you know why your mum would have gone up to Clough Bottom?"

He rubbed his good eye and shook his head. "She never went up there. She hated the place."

"Do you know why?" Rocco asked.

"She never said. I think it had something to do with the past."

"Do you know why Emily hated Clough Bottom, Mrs Mason?"

"It's *Miss*. I never married." She set a tea tray down and looked at Ricky. "Who told you that?"

"Mum always said she couldn't stand the place. We never went up there for picnics or anything when I was little."

"It's all in his head, Inspector," Enid insisted. "Emily had no reason to hate any place round here. It was her home, where she came from."

"Was Emily seeing anyone?" Calladine asked.

"No!" Enid sounded as if the idea was preposterous. "There's been no one for years. Not since she ditched that no-good husband of hers."

Ricky said nothing.

"Where did she work?" asked Rocco.

Enid turned to him. "She worked in the council tax department. It was a simple admin job, nothing complicated. She'd been there years."

"Have you ever heard of Jet Holdings?" Calladine added.

"No," she replied at once. "No idea. Why?"

"They were sending Emily money every month."

She didn't react but Ricky stared curiously at Calladine for a moment. Calladine got the impression that if his aunt hadn't been there, he'd have asked about it.

"It must be a company she worked for in the past, an investment, something like that." She looked nervously at Ricky as she spoke. Calladine suspected she wasn't telling them everything. Was she hoping the boy would keep his mouth shut?

"Tell me about Emily's ex-husband, Ricky's father," Calladine asked.

The woman shook her head. "He left them. I don't know why and I never pried," she practically whispered. "Look, Inspector. Do we have to talk about this now? Isn't Ricky upset enough already?"

"Do you see him, Ricky?"

The lad shook his head.

"Ricky hasn't seen his dad in years. The no-good waste of space never sent any money for him either. Emily raised him alone."

"How long since he left?"

"It's been seven, maybe eight years. He was real aggro, Inspector. Emily couldn't stand the strain. He'd stay out all night. He got into fights and mixed with a right bad crowd. Emily was thankful to be rid."

"Anyone in particular he fought with? Do you remember any names from that time?"

Enid Mason shook her head.

"Was Emily afraid of anyone? Had anyone made threats against her recently?"

"My goodness, no! We keep ourselves to ourselves, Inspector. We go to work and neither of us has ever mixed much. I don't think Emily had an enemy in the world."

Well, she had at least one, thought Calladine. The woman was being evasive. Did she have something to hide or was she simply protecting the boy?

"Did Emily have a mobile? We haven't found a handbag or a phone."

"She had a black shoulder bag. She kept her life in it, and her phone."

"You should ring the bank and cancel her debit or credit cards," Calladine advised. "Ricky, if you think of anything, or if Archer and his crew give you grief, let me know."

The lad nodded without much enthusiasm.

Suddenly there was an ear-splitting 'crack' from outside, followed immediately by another.

Rocco sprang to his feet. "That's gunshot!"

Calladine's pulse began to race. The DC had to be mistaken. The Hobfield wasn't perfect but there'd been no gun crime here for a long time. The two detectives went to the front door and stood on the deck. Below them a group of people were gathered around a figure lying on the concrete.

Ricky Blackwell came out onto the deck. "That's Wayne!" he gasped.

Calladine and Rocco raced for the stairs. They'd only been talking to the lad a matter of minutes ago.

"Has someone called an ambulance?" Rocco shouted, flashing his badge at the growing crowd.

Wayne Davey was lying on his back. They had heard him screaming but now he was only semi-conscious. Both legs were bleeding profusely.

"They've blasted his kneecaps, sir," Rocco whispered to Calladine. "Poor bugger."

Calladine pushed his way forward. "Did anyone see who did this?" Nothing but some vague mutterings. He bent down beside Davey. He was rambling, falling in and out of consciousness. "Who did this to you?"

Rocco tapped Calladine's shoulder. "The ambulance is here, sir."

"Speak to me, lad."

His eyes opened. They were glazed over. He must be in excruciating pain, thought Calladine. He doubted the boy'd say anything. This was a warning. His life was on the line and he wasn't stupid.

They waited until Wayne Davey had been taken away. "That limo's disappeared," he said to Rocco. "When we're back at the nick we must find out who it belonged to. And have a PC keep an eye on him at the hospital."

He looked around. The area had emptied suddenly. No one would talk. Davey had crossed someone, but who was it?

Calladine turned to Rocco. "That ambulance turned up bloody quick. Check on that too when we get back. I've a sneaking suspicion it was called out before the lad was shot."

* * *

"A shooting?" DCI Birch sounded incredulous. "Gang war, here in Leesdon?"

"Let's not get ahead of ourselves. It might be an isolated incident. We've had them before. The fact is, no one will talk to us — not yet anyway. Something is wrong on that estate. I'll go and see Wayne Davey in the hospital once he's come out of surgery. He might speak to me, given what's happened."

"Does Davey belong to a gang?"

"Highly likely. Most young men do. But the gangs on the Hobfield have been fragmented since Fallon's death."

"A fight for supremacy, then. Is that what we've got?"

It was a possibility. Just as Calladine was about to voice his opinion, Imogen interrupted.

"Sir! That car. It belongs to Rose Argent Enterprises Ltd."

Calladine felt his stomach tighten.

"*Costello.*"

He could see from the blank faces that the team didn't know the name, or what it meant. They'd not been in the force as long as he had.

Since the shooting, Calladine had been mentally sifting through the possible culprits. Potentially that included most of the Manchester underworld. But the name Vincent Costello hadn't even figured. The Hobfield was small fry. A villain like Costello wouldn't be interested.

"Costello is old school," he told the team. "He's made a fortune from his criminal activities. These days he hides under a veneer of respectability. His team have worked hard to airbrush out his dodgy past. But in his time he was a vicious killer."

"I've never heard of the man, sir," Rocco said.

"No reason you should have. He was long before your time, before mine too. He must be in his late sixties by now. His PR people have done a first-class job. The transformation into good guy has been so complete I almost believe the hype myself."

"And you think he's behind the shooting? You think he's making a play for the Hobfield?" Birch asked.

Calladine stuffed his hands in his pockets. He was thinking about what Wayne Davey had said. "Costello wouldn't be interested in that cash-starved estate. Word has been circulating for a while that he's retired. But if he did venture back into a life of crime, it would be something far more lucrative than a bit of dealing on the Hobfield."

"So why was that limo there?"

"I've no idea, ma'am. But we have to find out."

"I've found something, sir."

"Go on then, Imogen."

"Rose Argent is a sizable concern. It comprises a number of companies," she told them. "The accounts are up to date and filed each year on time. All of them are in the black."

"I'd expect nothing else," said Calladine. "These companies he runs, profitable are they?"

"Yes, sir. He's doing very nicely. He's certainly not short of a bob or two."

Calladine spoke to DCI Birch. "But don't be misled. Costello is a villain. Just because he's old and wealthy doesn't make him any less dangerous than he ever was. If, and it's a big if, this is down to him, we've got a huge problem. The man's past is so bloody the Hobfield would become a war zone."

"One of his cars was on that estate. You both saw it with your own eyes," Birch reminded them. "He'll have been sizing the place up."

"He doesn't need the aggro. The Hobfield isn't worth the effort. Not to a man like Costello."

Birch was looking at Imogen's screen. "This all looks fine to me."

"Of course it does," said Calladine. "His life today will be totally above board. He's clever. I don't believe he wants the Hobfield but I'm not taken in. His organisation may be big and profitable, but it's nothing but a smokescreen for his murderous past. Despite the big house in the country, the private school for the kids, he's still a capable villain."

"So what are we missing? What would he gain from running the Hobfield?"

"Nothing that I can see, ma'am. But if he was involved in that shooting today, then it sends the case spiralling into a whole new dimension."

"Perhaps he's being challenged."

"No one would dare. He might stay in the background these days but he still heads one of Manchester's largest and most prolific gangs." Calladine scratched his head. "He has his own security team. If there was any challenge it would be quashed at birth.

"Perhaps someone wants us to think it was Costello," Rocco suggested.

"We're back to that limo. It is registered to his company," said Birch.

Calladine was still puzzled. "It would have to be something big to drag him into the limelight again."

"So what could have brought him to our patch?" Rocco asked.

"It's vacant after the demise of Ray Fallon," Birch pointed out.

"That's not nearly enough," Calladine told them. "It has to be about something else."

Rocco was studying the information on Imogen's screen. "It was alleged that he was behind that bank robbery in Cheshire about a year ago. The gang got away with an absolute fortune."

"That was merely speculation, DC Rockliffe," Birch said. "Nothing was proven against him. We can't know for sure that Costello was behind that robbery."

Calladine sighed. "Nothing is ever proven against him, ma'am. Costello is a past master at getting away with things. He greases palms and intimidates. Cross him and you're dead. He has a team of goons to do his dirty work and an expensive brief by his side at all times. Central used to call him 'Fortress Costello.'"

"I remember CID at Central talking about it at the time," Birch said. "They suspected Costello. Someone leaked information to the local police. A member of his gang was suspected. Problem was, the witness disappeared without trace so no charges could be brought against Costello. I recall he was interviewed though."

"Do we know who that gang member was?"

"No, Inspector. Whoever gave the information didn't give a name."

"So why the Hobfield — and why now?"

"Because it's going begging, Inspector." Birch spoke as if it was simple logic. "He knows that if he doesn't step in then some rival outfit will."

"What puzzles me is how a young scally like Wayne Davey attracted his attention."

"He either wouldn't play ball or he's crossed Costello in some way," Rocco suggested.

Imogen turned to them. "That Cheshire robbery. There were two fatalities and a number of gang members injured. Because of the information given, armed police were waiting at the scene. One of the robbers was shot dead and one died later in hospital."

"And they still got away with the money?"

"Yes, Rocco. According to the report, the money was got out through the cellar and taken into the shop next door," Imogen told him. "The police made arrests. A small amount was recovered on one of robbers fleeing the scene. Amidst all the mayhem, the bulk of it was spirited away in a refuse truck."

"Is that relevant?" Birch asked.

Calladine had no idea. But if it was down to Costello he would be damned annoyed at the leak. And he wouldn't want to be in the informant's shoes either.

"Let me have a look at his record," Birch said to Imogen. "See what we're up against."

"There is nothing, ma'am. He's spotless. He's been arrested on a number of occasions and he's always walked clean away. There are either no witnesses or his alibi is cast iron."

"This one is the real deal, ma'am," said Calladine. "He's a far better operator than Fallon ever was. Fallon was a hothead. He got it wrong many times and ended up in prison. But not Vinny Costello. He always gets it right. That man has got away with everything from petty crime to murder, and there is never anything we can pin on him."

"If he is responsible for maiming that lad today, then we will nail him, Inspector," she insisted.

"I didn't realise he was local." Birch was looking at his record. "Born on the Hobfield too. Do you remember him, Calladine?"

"No, ma'am. He's quite a bit older than me. But I do remember him being talked about."

"Have you considered that that could be the reason he's back? It's his old stomping ground?"

"That would make him sentimental. Believe me, ma'am, Vinny Costello is a long way from being soft-hearted."

"He, or one of his people, was driving an expensive limo."

Calladine nodded.

"Then he'll have been seen. Someone pulled that trigger and to do that he had to get out of the car and walk across the square."

"You're spot on, ma'am, but naïve about the Hobfield, if you don't mind me saying. No one on that estate will dare speak up. They'll have been warned. They're not stupid. If anyone dares to breathe a word, Costello will take them out too. He is not someone you mess with." He turned to Imogen. "Did you check on that ambulance?"

"Yes, sir. It was called a good ten minutes prior to when you said the shooting occurred. A male voice reported that there had been a shooting on the Hobfield, and then hung up."

"Do they have the caller's number?"

"Yes. An unregistered pay-as-you-go mobile."

"See, ma'am? This is how it is. We end up with nothing."

"Nonetheless, Calladine, I want you to talk to him. If he was on that estate today, we want a statement. We'll bring him in."

"You must not do that!" A woman's voice shouted from the office doorway. "You can't drag Costello in here."

All eyes turned to look at the person who'd had the nerve to contradict Birch. For someone who sounded so full of authority, she certainly didn't look the part. She had long red hair scraped back into a ponytail and was wearing jeans and a hooded top. She looked like a kid you'd find hanging out on some street corner.

"Currently all dealings with Costello must go through me." She walked into the room. "Apart from which, I don't think he was responsible."

Birch turned and stared at the woman who'd had the temerity to call the shots in her nick. "We'll take this to my office now," she glowered. "Calladine, you come too."

Chapter 4

"Are you sure we've done the right thing, Jack? It needs a lot of work." Annie Naden looked around her at the interior of Clough Cottage. It was an utter mess. "Kids have been in here. Look at the empty beer cans and rubbish on the floor." She aimed a hearty kick. "The garden's a state too." She walked to the window. "What have they been doing? It looks like someone has been digging out there."

Her husband put an arm around her waist. "We used to be the same. Remember that old barn down Hopecross way? We used to tramp all the way up there, play our music, drink and generally trash the place."

"We were never this bad. Look, someone's even had a go at lifting the flags in here." The kitchen floor was still covered in the original Yorkshire stone.

Jack stamped in an effort to level one of them. "They'll make a lovely feature cleaned up."

"Keeping it traditional then, are we?"

Jack nodded. "I could even put an old range back in if you want. I know where there's one going begging."

She laughed. "Don't think we need to go that far. I'll have a range, but a brand-new gas one, please."

"When do you want to start?"

"The sooner the better. I'm sick of living with your parents." Annie began to wander through the ground floor rooms.

Walking behind her, Jack Naden nodded. "We'll get it cleaned up a bit and live here while we fix it up, if you want."

"What about water?" she asked. "We'll have to get our supply from the spring, but that well out there needs attention."

"We'll need to sort that as well as the pumps and pipework. Don't worry. My dad will help. We can copy the system he has up at the farm."

Annie led the way into the sitting room. "Look at this! It had beautiful panelling on the walls in here but the little sods have kicked holes in it."

Jack Naden ran his hand over the oak finish of the wall. "There's a cupboard in this panel," he said, pushing slightly. It swung open, revealing a small space behind it.

The air was suddenly full of dust, making Annie cough.

"Look at that!"

Annie peered forward through a haze of dust. In the bottom of the cupboard lay a school satchel. Her husband bent forward and lifted it out.

"Something the kids didn't find and ruin. It's one of those old-fashioned leather ones. Look! It has those shoulder straps so it can be worn on the back."

"It's filthy," Annie said, brushing off some of the dirt. "There's a name on the front. It's been written on a piece of card and stuck into the see-through pocket. I can't make it out."

"It must have been there years. It'll have belonged to someone long gone." Jack pushed back the panel. "Perhaps someone who lived in the cottage at one time."

"Do you think there's anything inside it?"

He gave the thing a shake, raising a cloud of dust. "Books, probably." He handed it back and walked away towards the kitchen.

Annie knelt on the floor and opened up the satchel. "The schoolbooks are still inside!" she shouted to her husband. "They're in really good condition too."

Annie took them out one by one. All the exercise books had covers made of wallpaper. She smiled. Her teachers had made them do the same. She read the name on the inside of the satchel: Carol Rhodes. Annie wondered if she was still around in the area, perhaps she could give it back. Her parents-in-law might know. They had lived for nearly fifty years in the farm a few hundred yards away.

There was nothing of much interest in the books. Carol obviously hadn't been a particularly good student. Her work was covered with scathing comments in red ink. Annie was about to give up when she spotted another smaller book tucked into a pocket. It was a diary.

It was pink with a lock that had long since rusted away. Annie flicked it open. The writing was in thick black pen and was easy to read.

Annie couldn't help feeling guilty. She was prying into the world of a teenage girl who'd long since grown up. This was her diary, her personal world, and these were her secrets. How would she feel about someone reading her diary?

Carol Rhodes was now probably old enough to be Annie's mother. But she'd been only fifteen years old when she'd written this. Back then, her head was full of clothes, boys and leaving school. No thought of staying on in education in those days. Apparently a job had already been earmarked for her at Leesdon paper mill. The entries rambled on at length about how she couldn't wait to leave that summer and what she'd do with the money. A holiday: 'Spain' was circled in red with the letter 'E' beside it. 'E' featured on almost every page. She must have been

Carol's best friend, or a boyfriend perhaps. They were going to a concert — a pop group Annie had never heard of were playing in Oldston. Then Annie spotted the hearts, two of them. One had 'Caro' and '?' written inside it; the other, 'E' and 'Ken.'

She wrote every day, pages of the stuff. Then suddenly it stopped. After the sixth of May 1969 Caro wrote no more. The last entry was simple. It read: 'pregnant.'

* * *

"Who was she?" Rocco asked Imogen, his mouth still open. "She's got some balls, ordering the DCI about like that."

"She'll be the DCI we've been promised from Daneside," Imogen told him. "She's here to help with the murder. I reckon the Costello angle has got them all fired up. I bet he's the real reason she's here."

"What has Costello got to do with Emily Blackwell's murder?"

"Nothing. But if Costello is currently operating on our patch, then Daneside and the new MIT would be interested. And they'd want to watch him," Imogen explained.

"She didn't sound like Daneside to me. That was a Yorkshire accent."

"So? What does it matter where she's from?"

Joyce interrupted. "Did you give the inspector his message?"

"No, I forgot." Imogen read the note on her pad. It was from Ruth Bayliss, the detective sergeant who usually worked with Calladine. "Ruth knows how fraught things get. She'll understand. Did she say what she wanted him for?"

"No. Just that it was important."

"She'll be missing us," Rocco piped up.

"I doubt that. Ruth'll have her hands full. It's no picnic looking after a tiny infant, you know," Joyce said.

"How hard can it be? They eat, sleep a lot and you push them around in a pram." He shrugged. "Piece of cake."

"I'd like to see you coping, Rocco."

"Well, he couldn't, could he?" Imogen smiled. "He's all talk, this one."

"I'll ring her later," Joyce told them. "Tell her what we're up to."

"What d'you reckon then, about the redhead? Trouble, or what?" Imogen asked.

"I'm sure she'll be okay once we get used to her," said Rocco.

A pretty face, thought Imogen. Typical. "She won't be okay if she persists with that attitude. DCI or not, Birch won't like being put in her place like that in front of the team. Personally, I think she's going to be a problem," she said.

* * *

"How can you be so sure Costello wasn't responsible for shooting that lad?" Birch asked the woman.

"Because my team had him under surveillance. He hasn't left his house in Harrogate for over a week. And that car — it wasn't his. It was a company car. Any one of his employees, or their family members, could have been driving it."

"Costello always takes a back seat while someone else pulls the trigger. It's called having other people do your dirty work." Calladine smiled glibly. "You must know that. You're not that naïve, surely?"

"If there's one thing I'm not, Inspector, it's naïve. It really pisses me off when male colleagues start with that sort of thing."

Birch cleared her throat. "My inspector saw the car himself," she told her.

"Did you see who pulled the trigger?"

Calladine shook his head.

"Then why blame Costello?"

"The *car*," Calladine repeated. "If Costello is staking his claim to the Hobfield and Davey crossed him, he would dive in with a gesture exactly like that. At the very least we should ask ourselves why the car was there. Can you explain why there was a shooting within minutes of it turning up?"

"No, and I'm not even going to try."

"I think you should at least give it a go, DCI . . . ?"

"King," she replied. "I'm DCI Eliza King, from the Yorkshire MIT. I've been seconded to the new MIT for Leesworth area for a while."

"We're not sure we are." Calladine smiled. "Party to anything I mean. The boys upstairs haven't decided yet."

"Well, I'm here regardless."

"Because of the murder or because of Costello?"

She didn't answer him.

"We don't like riddles, DCI King," Birch told her. "This is a shooting on our patch, so we will investigate. Currently we're investigating a murder too. DI Calladine will interview anyone he considers has something to offer."

"You are wasting your time. I know where Costello has been for every hour of last week. Why bring him in to have him laugh in your faces? He'll make you look like a bunch of bloody fools. And do you want to know how he'll do it?" She waited, her hands on her hips, and her dark eyes moved from one to the other. "He'll feed you some tale about that car being stolen and he'll provide a police report to prove it. I don't want to get heavy about this, but I will if you don't back off."

Her attitude rankled both Birch and Calladine. This was their nick. Birch's expression said it all.

"So we leave him alone, do we?" Rhona Birch said. "We just let him shoot and terrorise the people of Leesdon?"

"That won't happen. My team won't let it."

"It is already happening," Calladine said.

"We are gathering evidence that will finally nail him."

Calladine snorted. "Fat chance of that. It's been tried before and it failed." He paused, studying the woman. "You do know who you're dealing with?"

No response.

"You are not helping, DCI King," said Birch. "DI Calladine has a point. You are here to support the investigation into the murder that took place today. That, surely, is your priority."

"Unless the murder has something to do with Costello," added Calladine. "Is that it? Do you suspect him of killing Emily Blackwell too?"

"No . . ." She hesitated. "But they both lived around here once and could have known each other."

"The shooting and the murder are two completely different matters," Birch told her. "We know a vehicle belonging to his firm was on the estate. If you have explored any links between him and Emily, you should tell us what you've found."

"Can't," Eliza King said. "Not yet anyway."

Dislike was written all over Rhona Birch's face. "We don't have time for this," she told King.

"I'm here because of the murder," she insisted. "About the shooting — I don't know yet. That happened while I was still on the M62. I've only just caught up with events. Superintendent McCabe suggested Emily Blackwell might have known Costello and told me to keep an open mind."

"So why would he kill her?" Calladine asked.

"I've no idea." She looked at Calladine. "And it wasn't him personally, because I know exactly where he was."

"But you acknowledge that he could have been behind it," Birch added. "I repeat, it was one of his cars at the scene. That given, you can't go getting upset when Calladine drags the miscreant in."

"That would ruin months of work." Eliza looked at Birch and then at the DI, her eyes narrowing angrily. "We want Costello. He is top of our hit list. He's being monitored and he's unaware of it. I don't want him rattled."

"*You* want him! He's a Manchester villain. If any force is hounding Costello then it should be us."

"For the last few years his people have been running a drug-dealing operation on the East Yorkshire coast. We've taken down three of them. They were crucial but we need Costello. Only then will the gang become fragmented enough for it to cease existence."

Calladine shook his head. "You're fooling yourself. Costello is a sharp operator, sharper than a lot of detectives." This was pointed. "Are you sure he's not running rings around you?"

She gave him a look. Her eyes flared.

"Look, let's all calm down, shall we?" Birch said.

Calladine could see that King wasn't happy. She'd obviously expected to swan in here and just take over. Well, that wasn't going to happen. He'd have to know a lot more about her first. How much experience did she have in dealing with villains like Costello? The woman looked so young. Eliza King was wearing denim jeans, a hoodie and a pair of what he knew to be expensive Converse trainers. He'd bought Zoe a pair just like them at Christmas. Practically all the female DCIs he'd met so far were in the style of Birch — suited and smart. This one looked as if she'd be more at home on the Hobfield!

Calladine watched King move over to the office window. He would really like to know how a young woman like her had made DCI already. What was she? Late twenties, early thirties? Certainly no more than that.

"What is your role while you're with us?" Birch asked. "We have a murder and the shooting to investigate. We're one officer down, so we need all the help we can get."

"That's what I'm here for." Eliza King shot Calladine a wary look. "But Costello must be left alone. For the time being anyway."

"But why?" Calladine reiterated.

"Blunder into this and months of work will go down the tubes." This was said with feeling.

"Will you share what you've got on him?"

"No. It would serve no purpose at this time."

"So, shooting or not, he's free to do as he pleases."

"No. Our efforts are about to pay off, Inspector. Finally we have someone who will testify against him. Until we have all the evidence in the bag, we leave Costello well alone."

Calladine shook his head. "The reality is, you have nothing. You're here on a wild goose chase." He could scarcely believe what he was hearing. "Why do you think anyone would forfeit their life to help the police?"

"Costello is losing his grip. Something has happened to shake things up."

"Want to elaborate?"

"No. Perhaps a little further down the line."

Calladine suspected she had no idea. She was here on a fishing trip.

"If he's operating in Yorkshire, why are you chasing an informant in our neck of the woods?"

"Because this is where he lives," she told him patiently.

"There you have it, Calladine. The Hobfield connection."

"I'm still not sure, ma'am. I'm curious why someone from Leesdon would contact the Yorkshire force to squeal about Costello. Did McCabe enlighten you?"

Eliza King was still angry. "All you need to know is that we have an opportunity to get him. You don't want to be the detective who puts a spoke in that particular wheel, do you? Where the informant comes from is totally irrelevant."

Calladine tried another tack. "You have to trust us. You will need help. At the very least Costello or one of his people was witness to a shooting today."

She turned towards him, her expression hard. "I know he's a villain. The bastard kills people. He ruins lives." Now there was hatred in her dark eyes. "No one wants him locked up more than I do."

That look spoke volumes. "This is personal, isn't it?" Calladine looked at Birch. Surely she must see it too? "Personal means mistakes. What is it between you and Costello?"

"Now you're being dramatic, Inspector," Birch intervened with a half-smile.

"You're here because your little project is in danger of failing, isn't it? You have a problem." He was guessing. Eliza King's face remained impassive. "That's what's really pissed you off. That's what's brought you here. Someone's stopped playing ball."

"This isn't a game, Inspector," she snapped back. "You can sit there and make up fairy tales all day. But I won't tell you any more than I already have. The informant makes contact through me. You have to back off."

"Look at the Fallon case," said Calladine. "You have heard of Ray Fallon, I take it?"

She nodded.

"That was meticulously planned. An informant determined to give evidence was put into witness protection. But Fallon found out and had the poor bugger killed." Eliza King said nothing. "Costello will be aware of every move you make. God help anyone you rope into this because if Costello is anything like Fallon then you'll never even get close."

Eliza King gave him a filthy look. "We don't do things that way. My force has done its homework. We've kept this operation tight. I was transferred to Daneside specifically to wind this up."

She's shown her hand, thought Calladine.

"Not the murder, then? You are looking for someone on our patch."

"I can't say."

"Does the poor sod know you're coming for him?"

She nodded. "Arrangements have been made. Our informant will be in witness protection very soon."

"So where is he now? Wandering the streets of Leesdon, jumping out of his skin at every shadow?" He could see that Birch was wrestling with her temper. She was as disturbed as he was by what Eliza King was telling them.

"Will you need help?" Birch asked her.

"If I do, I'll ask. Superintendent McCabe promised me your full cooperation."

"There is still the shooting to clear up."

"DI Calladine is right," said Birch. "I still think someone should be interviewed about that." Birch met the DCI's gaze. "Costello will think it odd if he is not approached. It was definitely his car on that estate this afternoon."

Eliza King seemed to be considering this. "One of his people, Gavin Trent," she said, handing Birch a card. "He rang me a while ago. Costello was interviewed after a robbery and wanted to sue for harassment. We sorted things out. He seems like a reasonable guy. Ring him and he'll set things up. But if he spins you a yarn then accept it — for now." She turned to Calladine. "Speak to him only about the shooting, nothing else. Do you understand?"

And Eliza King walked out of the room.

Calladine looked at Birch and exhaled. "A force to be reckoned with, that one."

"I'm just as much in the dark as you are," Birch said. "But she's only with us until the end of this week, so I've been told."

That was a relief. It meant she wouldn't be on their backs for long. "The Emily Blackwell case has to be our priority, ma'am, followed by the shooting. I was on the Hobfield speaking to the victim's son when Wayne Davey was shot. Despite what that harridan out there thinks, Costello has to be approached. We will speak to everyone who was out and about on the estate at that time. His car was parked in full view. There is no way we can ignore that."

"I agree . . . but please don't refer to her as a 'harridan.' She is a DCI and therefore your senior. Grit your teeth and give her at least a modicum of respect."

But Birch was smiling.

He smiled back. "Softly-softly it is."

Chapter 5

"You're going to need somewhere to work."

Eliza King was pacing the corridor, deep in conversation on her mobile phone. He smiled. "Currently we have a spare desk in the incident room."

Pocketing her phone she followed him in.

"It won't do. The stuff I'm working on is . . . sensitive. I need a space of my own. Who's in there?" She nodded towards the door of Calladine's office.

"Me."

She put her hand on the back of Ruth's chair. "The empty desk here?"

"Sergeant Bayliss is on maternity leave," Joyce told her.

"There you are then — sorted. You can take this desk for now, DI Calladine, and I'll have your office. It won't be for long."

Calladine opened his mouth.

"I've brought my own laptop. Tell your techie people I'll need to connect to your network," she said to Joyce. "And if there's a cup of tea going, I wouldn't say no. I'll be at my desk."

"Is she going to call the shots on the Blackwell case now, sir?" Rocco asked.

"Officially she is," Calladine replied. "But whatever she gets up to it won't impinge on what we do."

There was a general sigh of relief.

"I want more background on Emily," he told the team. Calladine was trying to concentrate on the incident board and its scant information but he couldn't get Eliza King out of his head. He thought he'd worked out how she'd made DCI so young. She'd clawed her way up, kicking all rivals in the teeth as she went. He found himself smiling. She was some tough cookie. Nevertheless, she was a problem they could do without. She'd said she suspected a connection between Emily and Costello. Calladine couldn't think what, but it gave them something else to think about.

"Rocco and I went round and spoke to her sister. I don't know about you, Rocco, but I got the impression Enid Mason was being evasive."

Rocco nodded.

"There's a story there and I think it has something to do with Emily's ex-husband. And that money she got paid each month. We need to get the background on that."

"I'll do some digging on the system," Imogen volunteered.

"Her ex is Ken Blackwell. Rocco and I will go back to the Hobfield, make our presence felt." He checked his watch. "It's gone seven now, so it'll be tomorrow. We'll take a couple of uniforms. I'll talk to anyone who knew Wayne Davey — Kayne Archer in particular. Rocco, you speak to Emily's neighbours. Find out what you can about her private life. Imogen, speak to her employers. Try and find out who her friends were. We need to know why she went up Clough Hill and who with."

"I'm still trying to find out about that woman, Mrs Mallon, who bid for the cottage. She's a bit of a mystery. I know she didn't buy it but she tried hard enough."

"Talk to the auctioneers again. They should have her details. For now we'll call it a day. Rocco, I'll meet you outside the Hobfield community centre at eight tomorrow morning."

Joyce handed him a scrap of paper. "Message for you, sir, from Ruth."

"Urgent . . . I'd better drop by on my way home."

* * *

Ruth Bayliss flopped back onto her sofa. "If I don't get some sleep soon, I'll go mad," she groaned. "All he does is cry. I'll swear he can cry round the clock. Jake's impervious, he can sleep through anything, but not me. Every little whinge and I'm wide awake."

"He's cute though, isn't he?" Tom Calladine was watching the wriggly bundle on Ruth's rug.

"Oh he's cute alright, but the lungs on him! I was under the impression that babies slept all the time. I mean, how are you supposed to know? I've got no idea what to do. It's not as if they come with a 'quick start' guide or anything."

"Why not get him ready, stick him in his pram and I'll take him for a walk. I'm told I could do with the exercise and you can get your head down for an hour."

She grinned. "You are looking a bit out of condition. Too many pies."

He threw a cushion at her. "You've got some cheek!"

"Mind you, I'm not one to talk. I could do with getting into shape myself."

"You've got an excuse." Calladine stroked the infant's cheek. "Rocco was telling me about a new gym in town. I might give it a go."

"That's not a bad idea. I might just join you. I'm ready to squeeze my lumpy bod into lycra if you will too. What d'you say? We can suffer together."

"Okay, you're on, but you can forget the lycra."

Calladine was grinning as he rummaged through a pile of baby clothes. It felt like old times talking to Ruth like this. He wished he had her at his side on the case. She'd sort out the Yorkshire madam. "Will this do?" He'd found what appeared to be a padded onesie.

"Yep, perfect. Give him here." She held out her arms. "Are you sure you've got time for this? Haven't you got work to do?"

"It's piling up. One murder and a shooting on the Hobfield, and that's just today."

Ruth started to dress her son. "We haven't had one of those since Richard Pope. What's going on?"

"I'm not sure. But the name Costello is being bandied about."

Ruth frowned. "Vinny Costello?"

Calladine nodded.

"That is bad news. We don't want him running the Hobfield."

"I'm not sure he is. But something is going on."

"You can always pop round and run stuff past me. I feel so out of things, stuck at home."

"I might just do that. I'm going to need a sounding board. We've had a DCI from Daneside or the Yorkshire force thrust on us. One Eliza King. Proper handful she's shaping up to be. Easily irritated and doesn't want to share information. What are we supposed to do with that?"

"I'll remind you of those words when you get the hots for her."

"That won't happen. For starters she's only a child."

"Come off it, she's a DCI."

"Well, she looks like a child, a damn scruffy one too."

"Daneside, you said?"

"Officially she's from Yorkshire on secondment to Daneside, and now with us. I know what this is, can't kid me. No one can cope with the little madam. So they hand her around like pass the parcel."

"Why do you need another DCI?"

"We don't. She's here on a mission of her own, something to do with Costello. Eliza King thinks she's going to bring him in."

"Does she know who she's dealing with, Tom? You have warned her?"

He shrugged. "I have done my best, but she's not the type to listen."

"Costello has been quiet for a long time. What is it she's got on him?"

"An informant — who *might* be persuaded to give evidence."

"She needs to watch her step."

"Too bloody true she does."

Ruth changed the subject. "We've decided to have him christened. Harry John Ireson will be baptised at Leesworth Parish church this Sunday. That's what was urgent and why I rang the nick. I would have given you more notice but you're a devil to contact, Tom Calladine."

"Does that mean I'm invited?"

"Of course you are. But not only that. Jake and I would like you to be Harry's godfather."

Calladine was touched. "I've never been a godfather before. Are you sure I won't make a mess of it?"

"You'll be fine." She chuckled. "Even you can do it. It's easy. You come to the service in your best suit and you repeat a few lines the vicar will tell you, and that's it. There will be a bit of a bash after. At the Wheatsheaf in town, in their function room at the back."

"Who else is coming?"

"The world and his wife, Tom. Family, friends and I've asked our crowd from work, plus Doc Hoyle and some folk from the Duggan. But you could do with a plus-one."

"Who do you suggest? I was seeing Tasha Barrington but I don't think she's keen."

"You can ask Eve," Ruth told him firmly. "She'll be pleased, and I was going to ask her anyway."

"She's my mother. Won't be much fun, will it?"

"It's a christening. It's not meant to be *fun*. Only joking!" Ruth smiled.

"There we are, baby boy. All ready." She laid him in his pram and wheeled it over to Calladine. "Thanks for this, Tom. I really appreciate it. With a bit of luck Jake will be home when you get back. If he is, just hand him over. I'll probably still be asleep." And she yawned. "Here's your official invitation. The vicar wants us to have a practice before Sunday, so I'll let you know."

"Come on then, young master Ireson. Let's give Leesdon Park a whirl."

Pushing a pram was a new experience for Calladine. His daughter Zoe had been brought up by her mother in Bristol and he'd missed all the childhood stuff with her. It was about seven thirty in the evening but at this time of year the nights were long and light. He wandered down Leesdon High Street, making for the park, when he almost bumped into Eliza King coming out of the supermarket.

"Yours?" she asked doubtfully, peering into the pram.

"No. He belongs to my sergeant, Ruth Bayliss. I'm giving her a break."

She gave him an odd look.

"Have you found somewhere to stay?" he asked.

"Yes. The pub further down." She gestured to the Wheatsheaf.

"It's a bit rough there. You won't get much peace and quiet."

"Just as well I don't sleep much then, isn't it?"

She had an answer for everything.

She was clutching a packet of crisps and a bottle of cola.

"Is that your tea?" he asked.

"I don't go a bundle on healthy eating. Work's so full on, I'm usually too busy. Is there anything else you'd like to know, Inspector, before I crack on?"

Keep out of my business and leave me alone. It came through in everything she said.

"I was just being friendly," he said.

"Well, you'd be better off making friends with someone else. I don't do friends. They take up too much time."

"Shame. This is a friendly town. The team are an okay bunch too. We should try to get on. We are working together."

"No we are not. I'm here on a case that has to do with the Daneside and Yorkshire forces. I'd appreciate you keeping out of it."

"That's me told," he said.

"Look, I don't mean to come across as a narky bitch. It's just how I am. You can take it or leave it. I come to work to do exactly that — work. I don't intend to stay round here long and I'm not interested in making friends. Polite conversation is frankly boring and I've got a report to write tonight. So if you don't mind, I'll let you get on with your stroll."

* * *

Eliza King knew that if she wasn't careful DI Calladine would be all over her case like a rash. He was as keen on putting Costello away as she was. But she wasn't going to let that happen. This particular criminal was her catch.

He'd been right about the pub, though. It was a dump. The room they'd given her was straight out of the seventies. Even two floors up, she could still hear the music and the shouting coming from the bar.

She took her phone and tapped in a number. "Becca? You okay, love? How did you get on?"

"Difficult, Mum, and I was a bag of nerves. I don't like exams and this was GCSE maths. It was hard."

"You'll have done alright, you always do. Look at the marks you got in the mocks, they were brilliant. How's your sister?"

There was a silence.

"She's gone out with him again — Harvey," Rebecca King finally admitted. "There was nothing I could do to stop her. She was being a right cow."

Eliza's heart sank. "It's not your fault. Did he come round? Jade didn't let him into my house, did she?"

"No. He rang her and arranged to meet. She's hardly been home at all. It was four this morning when she got back from last night. She stunk of booze and hardly said two words to me. I think Jade's drinking too much. She said I wasn't to tell you. Before she left tonight, she gave me a tenner and made me promise to keep my mouth shut."

"She never learns," Eliza said bitterly. She was angry. This was the first time she'd left her daughters. It wasn't something she'd do ordinarily, but the Costello case was so important she'd had no choice. She'd made her eldest daughter, Jade, promise to stay at home. She was almost nineteen and Eliza was relying on her. It was obviously asking too much. Where Harvey Evans was concerned, the girl was blind.

Jade simply didn't understand how important her mother's work was. Eliza was a single parent and it was her work that fed and clothed them all. She'd had her daughters young. She was thirty-eight years old but looked much younger. All she asked was that Jade meet her halfway and do as Eliza asked when it mattered.

"When are you coming home?"

"I won't be back until the weekend. Becca, you can't stay in the house on your own. If Jade doesn't come home within the next hour, get Alison to stay over." Alison was the daughter of a neighbour and Becca's friend. "I'll ring Jade and see what she's playing at. If I don't get anywhere with her, you'll have to go to Auntie Sarah's. I'm sorry, love. You shouldn't have to cope with this on top of the exams."

"It's okay, Mum. But Jade's turning into a right problem. Earlier, well, she was like before — you know, when she was ill. She was all edgy and pale, a real bag of nerves. She seemed to calm down when he rang."

And Eliza knew exactly why that was, although she didn't want to discuss it with Becca. She had enough on her plate with the exams. Jade was weak. She'd fought one battle with drug addiction and come through it. But now she was falling into the abyss again. Becca would be devastated if her big sister put them through all that again.

"I've got some work to do but I'll ring before you go to bed. Lock up tight and don't forget to feed the cat."

Eliza rang Jade straight away. When the girl eventually answered her speech was so slurred Eliza could barely understand her. "Where the hell are you? You are supposed to be at home with Becca!"

"Keep your hair on." Jade giggled drunkenly. "Me and Harvey are out. We're having a good time. Something you could do with having yourself!"

"Mind your tongue. Control yourself. You promised me, Jade. You said you could do this." Eliza knew she was wasting her time. The girl was off her head. "Why him? Why put us all through that again? You know he's no good. All he wants is to get you hooked on that stuff. Why don't you see what he is?"

"Because I like him!" Jade was shouting down the phone. "You always try spoil things. Becca's a big girl now. She can look after herself. She's not daft."

"She's sixteen! What if something happens? I take it you're not planning on going home tonight."

"For fuck's sake, Mother. Cut the umbilical cord! Me and Harvey are going back to his. I don't know when I'll be back — if ever! If you're so concerned about the kid, you shouldn't go working away. Should you?" And she rang off.

In a fit of rage, Eliza hurled the phone onto the bed. Jade had gone too far. She'd taken advantage of her mother's absence and there was nothing she could do about it.

Jade had been hit hard when Eliza had split with her dad three years ago. But it didn't help to know the reason why her eldest daughter behaved the way she did. Life chasing criminals was difficult enough without the aggro she got at home. Eliza had worked hard to get help for the girl. She even paid for her to go into rehab, but it made no difference. Within a month she was back on the drugs. And all because of Harvey Evans. He was her supplier. The bastard had been on her case right away. The problem was, his hold on Jade was now affecting her and Becca.

Her mobile rang again.

"We've lost contact with the target, ma'am," said a male voice. It was Dominic Shevlin, her sergeant. "We texted yesterday but suddenly he's dropped off the radar. The mobile we gave him and his own phone are both switched off."

"Damn! Do we have anyone watching him?"

"No. He's not been a problem up until now. He was just a phone call away, as arranged."

"He got scared. He could have been threatened."

"I don't see how, ma'am. We've kept everything tight this end."

She'd made a mistake. Eliza realised that she should have kept the man on a shorter lead, brought him in sooner. "I've been a fool," she admitted. "Now I'll have to go look for him. I've really ballsed this up, haven't I?"

"No, Boss. The informant came to us, remember? He wanted this. He offered us information. We had no reason to think he'd do one when things got tight."

He was right, but it didn't help. "Do me a favour, Dom. Look in on Becca on your way home. Jade's at it again."

Eliza didn't talk about her personal life as a rule, but she'd worked with Dom a long time and he'd sort of guessed. He was a good man and would never gossip to the team about her problems. He had enough of his own.

Despite having the informant's address, finding him could be challenging. Eliza didn't know this town. But if he'd got cold feet and done a runner, they were screwed. She'd no idea where he might hole up or who his friends were. She had asked but the informant was unwilling to offer anything other than the evidence she needed.

Eliza took a map of Leesdon from her briefcase and studied the network of streets. She traced over it with a finger. Got it: 'Grange Street.' This was the address he'd given. It was behind the hospital, so that's where she'd make for.

Eliza decided to walk. She stuck the map in a back pocket of her jeans just in case, and her police badge in the other. Slinging a hoodie over her T-shirt, she grabbed her mobile and left. Downstairs, the bar was busy. Several pairs of male eyes watched as she made for the exit. She was new, different and with an accent that wasn't local. No doubt she'd be the hot topic for the next few minutes.

Chapter 6

Eliza had only been here a matter of hours but it was long enough to know that she didn't like Leesdon. It had too many contrasts. It was battling with itself about what sort of place it was. On one hand it had any number of quaint, cobbled lanes full of stone cottages, some still with the historic weavers' windows up on the attic floor. They'd be much sought after. You would need a fair income to live in one of those, she was sure. But not far away were the terraced back streets, strewn with litter, scruffy kids playing in the road, all the obvious signs of poverty. And then there was the infamous Hobfield estate: built in the mid-sixties as an overspill estate to rehouse the folk who'd once lived in the terraced streets of Manchester. If it wasn't so close to the hills, Leesdon would have nothing going for it. But the Pennines were literally on the doorstep and lifted an otherwise decrepit town into something special.

Eliza lived by the sea on the East Yorkshire coast. After her divorce she'd wanted somewhere quieter for her girls, somewhere not contaminated with the memories of her toxic marriage. The village she'd chosen was a tranquil backwater, away from the resorts of Scarborough and Whitby. But given what was happening with Jade she'd still got it wrong. She'd not moved far enough away from Harvey Evans.

Grange Street was pleasant enough, two neat rows of terraced houses with their own parking spots. Eliza crossed her fingers that he hadn't lied about his address and knocked at number five. A middle-aged woman, who she took to be his mother, opened the door.

The woman looked her up and down. "Is your son in?" asked Eliza.

"No. Why? Who are you?"

"Just a friend." Eliza smiled. "He said to pop round if I was ever in town."

The look on the woman's face was doubtful. "I haven't seen him in weeks. And that suits me just fine."

Not what Eliza wanted to hear.

"So if you do find the toerag just be sure to tell him to stay away. Life's a helluva lot simpler without that waste of space under my feet." She banged the door shut.

This was bad. Eliza knocked again.

"I have to talk to him. Do you know where he hangs out, or a friend he might be staying with?" For the informant's safety, she did not want to broadcast the fact that she was police.

"No, love. I can't help." She looked at Eliza suspiciously. "I don't know what this is about, or who you are. But my advice is to stay away."

"This is really important," Eliza said.

"The last time I saw him he was with a crowd of his mates on the Hobfield. Try there. He'll be shacked up in some dump of a flat, high as a kite."

The Hobfield. Calladine territory. She might have no choice but to ask the DI for help.

* * *

Kayne Archer gave his mate a chilling smile and held the gun aloft. "This useful piece of kit will give us the edge we need. A present from our new benefactor. With his

56

help we're going to run the estate. Any aggro from Costello's mob, and this little beauty will help us sort it. There'll be no more shootings on our patch unless it's us pointing the gun." He passed it to Mick Garrett. "You need to learn how to handle it." His mate examined the weapon tentatively and he laughed. "Don't worry. It's not loaded."

"You're not serious, Archer?" said Mick. "I didn't get into this to do no killing. What happened to Wayne shook me up. The drugs are one thing, but guns . . ."

Archer smiled back. "Think of it as protection, then. Wayne getting it like that has shown us how much we need to stay on our toes."

"What do we do for bullets?" Mick asked.

"I'm seeing someone later. All arranged by the new big boss. For a trade, he'll provide all the ammo we need."

"What trade?"

"The weed. We supply him and in return, he'll supply us."

"Where did you get it — the gun?"

Archer tapped the side of his nose. "Told you, I was given it. We're not on our own anymore. We have friends who will provide."

"Come on. Where did it come from? Folk don't give guns away."

"Think of it as payment in advance," Archer told him.

"In advance of what?"

"The work we'll be doing. Work we'll get well paid for. Leave the questions, Mick. You knew what we were getting into."

"There's something written on here." Mick was examining the barrel. "I think it's a name. The letters are worn and old. Can this be traced?"

"No, fool, of course it can't." Archer snatched the weapon from Mick.

"If it belonged to someone else, it could get you into trouble."

Archer sneered. "You really are going soft. I reckon this baby will keep us *out* of trouble. The bloke who gave me this guaranteed it was clean."

"What bloke? Why don't I know him? You didn't nick it, did you?"

"Stop asking stupid bloody questions. I told you. We need the gun. This isn't a school playground. It's down to us to watch this patch."

"You must be mad. We can't take on Costello with one empty pistol. Is this new boss you're on about for real?"

"Look, Mick, he knows what he's doing. He'll make sure Costello has other things to worry about until we've got the estate sewn up."

"Used guns can be traced. It might have killed someone. We don't want the blame for that."

Archer pushed his face into Mick Garrett's. "I didn't pinch this and no one is coming looking. No one is getting blamed for anything. Understand? The people we're working for will watch our backs."

"As long as you understand that having that thing in your pocket puts us in a very different game."

"We'll talk later. I've got someone to see now." Archer checked the time on his mobile. "You've got work to do, haven't you? The weed won't sell itself."

"Who are you meeting?"

"Better you keep out of it for now."

Archer was reluctant to tell his mate too much. On one hand he could do with the back-up. Wayne Davey being shot like that was a blow he hadn't anticipated. But on the other hand there was money to be made and he didn't fancy sharing.

"Sure you don't want me to come along? Get your back?"

"It's best if you keep out of it."

"Don't say I didn't warn you."

* * *

By the time Archer reached the meeting place it was dark. He was nervous. He didn't like waiting and the man was late. Bar one other time, up until tonight they'd only communicated via the pay-as-you-go mobile he'd given him.

The meet had been the man's idea, as had the place — under the viaduct. Archer stood in the shadows cast by one of the huge stone pillars, where he couldn't be seen. For extra reassurance he kept a tight grip on the gun in his pocket. Didn't know and didn't trust. If things got heavy he'd get one in first.

"Archer!" a voice hissed. "You alone?"

Archer spun around. He couldn't see him properly. He too was in the shadows. The man was like him — wary. But he could tell that he was older, by a good few years, plus he was wearing a suit.

"Yeah, as agreed. What d'you want?"

"I want results." The man spoke into the darkness between them. "We had an agreement. You haven't kept to it."

"My mate Wayne got shot. It scared the hell out of me. It set us back. We're now a man down."

"What happened to Wayne was unfortunate. But things will settle. Costello won't win this. He's losing his edge. You have to keep your nerve. You just make sure everyone understands who's in charge around here. It's time you threw your weight about more. You'll get no arguments from me. Once Costello sees the estate is secure, he'll back off."

"Costello had Wayne shot?" Archer suddenly felt cold.

"He knows what's happening. What did you expect him to do?"

"Wayne didn't deserve that. Problem is, if the police push him, Wayne will talk. He'll drop us all in it."

"Then get on with the job and stop pissing me about."

"What happened to Wayne — it changes things. Makes things too risky. Perhaps you should up the payment."

"You're getting paid too much as it is."

"We can't take on Costello without resources. We need a show of muscle around the estate. More money and I can convince others to join us."

"Bad idea. Before we can blink we'll have a turf war on our hands. We do this quietly. We move in, take the lot and leave Costello wondering what happened. You've done everything I told you about the other thing?"

Archer nodded.

"Good. Word will have reached Costello by now. It'll give him something to worry about. Time to drop it. Don't contact the police again — got it?"

"I could get my head blown off for what I've done."

"Keep out of sight. Get the others to do the running."

"Getting shot wasn't in the agreement."

The man came a little closer. "Get on with what you're paid for and don't cross me, Archer."

"What if the police ask questions? They're bound to after what happened to Wayne."

The man grabbed him by the scruff of the neck. "You're winding me up. Don't become a liability."

"Let me go! I can't breathe."

Archer lowered his eyes. The man had half of his little finger missing on one hand. Archer was gasping but he couldn't take his eyes off it. How had that happened?

"So far you've done a good job. Keep your mouth shut and your head down, and we're onto a winner." Finally the man threw him to the ground.

"If the police ask questions, what do I tell them?"

"They know it wasn't you shot your friend. There's plenty of talk going round. They know Costello wants to come back and what he's capable of."

Archer took the gun from his pocket. "I don't want this anymore. If I'm picked up, and the police find it . . ." He pushed the gun towards the man.

"You need it. It might save your life. Go back to the flat and do what we pay you for." He handed Archer a couple of notes. "This will keep you going for a while."

Archer shook his head and put the gun back in his pocket. Two fifty quid notes. "That won't keep me for long."

"Be creative."

"I need more. I've got to pay Addy."

"Don't wind me up, kid. You don't want to end up like your friend Wayne."

A shiver flew down Archer's spine.

"I'll be in touch tomorrow. You wanted to be part of this. In means exactly that. You can't pick and choose." He grabbed hold of Archer again. "It's quite simple. You follow instructions. If you want to live."

And then he was gone. Archer watched him until he disappeared. He took the mobile from his pocket, removed the sim card and threw them both into the river. The man could stuff his plans. Taking on Costello was far too dangerous. After what happened to Wayne, he had no intention of hanging around.

"What you up to, Archer?"

It was Mick Garrett.

"What're you doing here?"

"I followed you," he replied. "You're up to something. I won't be sidelined. If there's a deal going down for the weed, then I'm in."

"Not here and not now, mate," Archer said, squinting into the gloom. "You'll get your share. We agreed — remember?"

"What you doing here?"

"None of your business. This is private stuff."

Garrett grabbed Archer's arm. "If you are going behind my back, I'll do you."

"Don't be stupid. The bloke I've just met will only deal with me."

"Is that the bloke who gave you the gun?"

"Wait in the flat. I'll come and find you in a while," said Archer.

"The police have been all over the estate. They won't be finished yet."

"The shooting wasn't down to us."

"You've got a gun, remember?"

"I didn't have it then, did I?" Archer hissed.

"So who shot him?"

"One of Costello's lot."

"You're a stupid bastard, Archer. We can't take him on. The man's evil. We'll all end up dead. The police will come looking, but they're pussycats compared to that one."

"Let the police look. We'll be fine. We didn't do for Wayne. Don't talk about the gun to anyone — got it?" Archer cast a furtive glance into the blackness. "I'll text you later. We'll meet up."

"No way. I'm getting out and so should you. If what happened to Wayne is down to Costello, then we'd be better off with the police on our backs."

"Keep your mouth shut, Mick."

"A disappearing act needs money."

"The weed's not ready yet. Addy will let me know and I'll be in touch."

"So we're broke. Where am I supposed to go, Archer?"

"I don't know. Use your head."

"You're up to summat. If you're double-dealing, squeezing me out of what I've earned, I'll make life difficult," said Garrett.

"It's not what you think. The bloke I met has nothing to do with you or Wayne. But he'll be pissed off if he finds out I've spoken to you."

"Be careful, Archer. If I find out you've dropped me in it, I'll tell the police everything I know."

"Just do one."

Archer watched his mate walk away. His figure blended with the shadows for a few seconds and then he was gone.

Chapter 7

Wednesday

"Oddly quiet, don't you think, sir?"

"It's only eight. Most of the folk on this estate are jobless. They lie in bed all morning sleeping off the night before."

Calladine and Rocco were sitting in the snack bar at the Hobfield community centre, drinking tea.

"Did you see Ruth?"

"I did as it happens. I took the baby out for a stroll last night so that she could get some rest."

"Are you missing her, guv?"

"Yes, Rocco. Work isn't the same without her, is it?"

"She'll be back before you know it. You know what she's like — can't stay away from the job."

Calladine shook his head. "Stiff competition, a baby."

Rocco smiled. "They do a mean bacon butty here. Just listen to the sizzle coming from behind that counter. Lift anyone's mood that."

Calladine swallowed his tea. "No time. We've got to go." Then he sniffed. The smell of frying bacon filled the room. "We might come back later, see how things go."

"Thought you might be on a health kick after yesterday, sir."

"So why tempt me with the prospect of bacon? I might do something with Ruth. She fancies the gym too. It's all about finding the time."

"You should go for it — the pair of you."

"We'll see. It's not come to that yet." But it was getting perilously close, he knew. He wasn't carrying his fifty-one years at all well. The sum total of his exercise was walking the dog down to the common and back each evening. What was that, half a mile? Not enough to stop the rot. Perhaps when this little lot was sorted he would try the gym. Couldn't do any harm, could it? He was due a health check anyway. He couldn't afford any problems. His job depended on it.

They walked towards the tower blocks.

"None of this makes any sense," Rocco said. "Why kill Emily Blackwell and why would someone like Costello target a scally like Wayne Davey?"

"Perhaps it wasn't down to Costello," Calladine replied.

"Then who?"

"Could be anyone. Some bloody fool making a play for the action and mistakenly thinking Davey was the rival to beat."

A cleaner at the community centre had told them that the squat was on floor ten of Egret House, the tallest of the blocks. The detectives decided to visit the flat together — safety in numbers. Then Rocco would go and speak to Emily's neighbours.

Calladine hauled himself up the last couple of floors. He was gasping, mouth open, chest aching. He leaned against the wall for a few minutes. His heart was pounding.

Rocco nodded. "Told you. You need to reel it in a bit."

Calladine was bent over, his hands on his knees, still breathing heavily. "I do a bit. I've got the dog now, the one I'm looking after for Marilyn."

Rocco chuckled. "Looking after! Marilyn's banged up for the foreseeable. That dog is yours now, sir. No wriggling out of it."

"Alright, I'll walk him a little further. But like I said, problem is finding the time."

"The booze, precious little exercise, you know the drill. I'm only saying because Ruth isn't here. She'd be on you like a ton of bricks if she saw you in this state."

"Has she been talking to you?"

"We talked last night. She didn't like the look of you yesterday."

So that's how it was. No Ruth, so Rocco was his appointed conscience. Ruth Bayliss had a lot to answer for. After he'd taken the infant off her hands too. "Next time, the pair of you can tell me to my face," he huffed.

Calladine was still panting as Rocco walked along the deck, banging on all the doors. The tenth-floor flats were mostly boarded up. They were allegedly part of the refurbishment programme, but it looked to Calladine as if the council had totally forgotten about them.

A lone voice shouted out from behind one of the doors. "Get lost!"

Calladine positioned himself outside. "Police. Kayne Archer in there?"

He heard the squeal of bolts and then the door opened an inch or two. A youth stuck his head out. He rubbed his eyes and yawned. From what they could see of him, he looked scruffy, in a stained T-shirt and ripped jeans.

Calladine smiled. "Kayne Archer or Mick Garrett."

"They're not here. They went out last night and didn't come back."

"Have you tried their phones?" Calladine asked.

"Neither of them's answering. Weird that. Usually they're never off the buggers."

"Are they living here?"

The lad shrugged.

Calladine didn't have time for this. "I can always drag you down to the station. See if that loosens your tongue."

The boy opened the door a little wider. A gust of hot air hit Calladine in the face. The smell was unmistakable.

"What's going on in there?" He tried to see past the boy but he moved, blocking Calladine's view.

"Archer's been here a week or so," he admitted. "Mick stays sometimes but he does go home."

"Shut the door!" bawled someone from within.

"Who else is in there?"

"There's only me and Beanie. Wayne's in hospital."

"And who are you?"

"Addy — Greg Addison."

"Well, Greg Addison, there is a distinct smell of cannabis wafting through your front door." Calladine nodded at Rocco and the two detectives pushed their way inside.

"You've no right . . ." The lad's attempt to block their way was half-hearted. He didn't look as if he had any fight in him.

"You Beanie?" Calladine spoke to a face peering around another half-open door leading off the room.

The lad nodded. Calladine could see intense light spilling through the gap at the bottom. "What have you got in there?"

He shook his head. His eyes darted towards his friend.

"Rocco, take a look."

Addison made as if to stop the DC but then thought better of it.

Rocco kicked the door open. The light was so bright it made them all blink. "They're growing the stuff!" said the DC.

The plants were everywhere, in huge pots all over the floor and on shelving around the walls. The heat and the smell were overpowering.

Calladine took out his phone. This pair would be taken in. "Who are you working for?" he asked.

"Ourselves. It's for private use," tried Addison.

"Come off it, lad. There's enough weed here to sort the entire town. This has taken some setting up." Calladine followed the wiring from the heaters fixed to the ceiling to its source. "Those are plugged into the mains. You paying the bill?"

Greg Addison shook his head. "We're taking it from the flat downstairs. It's empty but the lecky is still on."

Calladine's phone rang. He was expecting it to be the nick confirming they were on the way, but it was Birch.

"This is turning out to be some morning," she began. "A report has come in of a missing teenager. Ordinarily I'd leave it a while — he is nineteen. But his name is on the incident board. One Mick Garrett. Mean anything?"

"Yes. He's one of Archer's crew. What makes him missing?"

"Tearaway he might be in the daytime, but his mother likes him home nights. She rang in this morning. She's not seen him in two days and his mobile is turned off. She can't get hold of Archer either and thinks something is going on. Given what we know, she could be right."

"Problem is where to look. It looks to me as if they've gone to ground. I've found where Archer's been dossing down, Garrett too on the odd occasion, but neither are here now. I'm sending in two scallys from Egret House. They've been growing cannabis in an empty flat. I'll give them the third degree later."

"And DCI King has asked to speak to you."

"Has she said what about?"

"No, and I didn't ask. I'll tell her you've been delayed."

The two lads were leaning against a wall. Neither looked as if they'd seen any water or food in days. "You've been hard at it?" asked Calladine.

Addison shrugged. "Got to get the stuff right."

"Who are you doing this for?"

"It's a sort of co-op. We all get a share."

"Archer in on this?"

"He'll do me if I talk to you lot. He's not like the others — he's dangerous."

"Where is Archer? Do you know who his contacts are? Who is he seeing about this little lot?"

"He doesn't tell us anything. When he sells, we'll get a cut. That's all we're interested in. We've not seen him these last couple of days." He looked at Beanie, who nodded.

"What about Mick Garrett?"

Addison nodded again. "The same. He and Archer were dossing down in there." He indicated another room.

"We'll get forensics down here, see what they come up with."

* * *

The nurse looked up briefly from her desk at a porter pushing a wheelchair. "Bed six. He needs to go to X-ray."

The porter nodded and walked down the centre of the ward. In bed six was a man with a leg in plaster and next to him, the mark. He looked back. The nurse was on the phone, laughing.

The tall man parked the wheelchair between the two beds. Wayne Davey was half asleep.

"Wake up," hissed the man, shaking Wayne Davey's arm.

Davey groaned and opened his eyes.

"You're in a bad way." The man pulled the curtain around the bed. He gave Davey a cold grin. "That's what you get for being a naughty boy. Shame you had to cop a bullet. It was nothing personal. It could have been any one of you. You should have been less visible."

69

Davey had no idea who the man was or what he was talking about. He wanted to shout for help, but he couldn't. The anaesthetic had made his throat dry as sandpaper.

"You and your mates are a liability. You've got loose tongues, the lot of you. Mr Costello can't take any more risks."

Davey shook his head.

Another icy smile. "That's why you'll have to go. It's simply business. I stand to cop for a fortune if I get this right. If I don't . . ." He drew a finger across his throat. "If you were in my shoes, you'd do the same." He patted Davey's arm. "I've invested too much in this already," he whispered as if confiding. "I don't plan on failing, and I don't want any witnesses helping the police."

Davey's eyes were wild with fear. He really didn't have a clue what the man was on about and he was too petrified to ask. He'd never even seen him before. He wanted to get up, run for his life. He tried to inch out of the bed but he was stuck there. The plaster casts on both his legs saw to that.

The man lifted the blanket. Davey noticed with a shudder that he had half a finger missing. "Not much use to you now, or anyone else for that matter. The man peered out between the curtains. There was no one around. The bloke in the next bed was sleeping and the nurse wasn't at her desk. "I'll make it quick," he whispered, as if it was a kindness. "No hard feelings. Like I said, this isn't personal."

"No! You can't. I've done nowt! What d'you want?" Suddenly Davey'd found his voice.

The man laughed.

Davey closed his eyes. "Please. I'm no threat. What can I do in this state?"

"You can talk, lad."

He felt the weight of the pillow as the man pushed it down on his face. Wayne Davey was terrified, too weak to fight. He was gasping for air, his arms flailing about wildly as the knife slid between his ribs and into his heart.

Chapter 8

"My office!" Eliza King called out as soon as she spotted Calladine in the corridor.

"It's mine, actually."

She dismissed this with a wave of her hand.

He wasn't in the mood for a row and that's all she seemed to want. "How can I help?"

She closed the door behind them. "The Hobfield. Tell me about the place."

"It's deprived, forgotten, somewhere people don't talk about. It houses most of the criminals in this town. There used to be a pub there. Great fun on a Saturday night that place was." He chuckled. "Kept uniform in overtime for years."

"If I wanted to find someone, where would I look?"

"You'd have to tear the place apart. They stick together. Unless you've got some intelligence from uniform then it would be useless." He saw her face fall. "Why? Lost someone?"

She turned away. "Thank you, DI Calladine. You've been no help at all."

She had paperwork covering most of his desk. He could see a file marked 'Costello.' Calladine itched to get his hands on that, find out more about what she was doing here.

"Please tell me you've not lost your informant?"

Her face gave nothing away.

"This has nothing to do with your team."

"It might have. Wayne Davey was kneecapped and Mick Garrett appears to be missing — Archer too."

Eliza King looked startled. "Someone should have told me sooner."

"Why? Do those names mean something to you?"

"I don't want to discuss that until I know more."

"I suggest you keep your eyes on the incident board in that case. Everything we get will be on there."

"Do you have any idea where Archer and Garrett have gone?"

"No. They could be dead for all we know. Those lads have upset someone. The problem is — who?"

She didn't look happy. He was fed up with dancing around this woman's moods. "What have those young men got to do with your investigation, DCI King?"

"You're looking for him — Archer?"

No response.

"Why are you so interested? Is he your informant?"

"I want to speak to him. His name came up during our investigation into Costello's recent activities."

That could mean anything.

"Vinny Costello and Kayne Archer? Hardly, DCI King. Have you ever met Archer?"

She shook her head.

"He's an out-of-work scally off the Hobfield. Up until half an hour ago he was growing weed in an abandoned flat in one of the tower blocks. I'll give him some credit for being enterprising, but Costello? He'll never even have heard of the lad."

"Nonetheless his name came up."

"Want to tell me more?"

"No."

"There'll be a briefing in the incident room later to bring the team up to date. Join us if you wish."

"I've got work to do."

"We're not exactly dossing around drinking tea ourselves."

"When you get something positive be sure to let me know." She held the office door open for him.

"I wish you'd tell me why you think the murder and the shootings are linked," Calladine said as he was leaving. "It might help all of us."

Eliza King shook her head. "I don't know that they are."

"Joyce will put out a report of any findings later today. Plus the PM reports will come in very soon. Anything else — just ask." He walked out.

If Costello did mean to take over the Hobfield, he would need someone to run it. Not Kayne Archer — he wasn't bright enough. But whoever Costello appointed might want Archer on board. Calladine shook his head. He was still convinced that Costello wasn't be interested in the Hobfield.

* * *

Enid Mason didn't look pleased to see DI Rockliffe.

"I've told you everything," she insisted. "And I don't like the neighbours seeing police at my door."

He smiled at her. "Just a couple more questions."

She moved aside for him to come in.

"Do you know where Ken Blackwell is? Have you contacted him about Emily's death?"

"Yes, I've told him."

"So you do know where he is."

"He's doing a ten-year stretch in Strangeways, which is why I don't like to talk about him in front of Ricky."

"What's he in for?"

"Robbery — but he was carrying a gun. He's been in and out of prison most of his adult life. The man's a waste of space."

"Does Ricky know?"

"Yes, of course he does, but we don't ram it down his throat. All me and Emily wanted was for Ricky to stay this side of the law. There is so much temptation on this estate, Detective. You've no idea."

He smiled. "Oh, I think I have. Have you ever heard the name Vincent Costello?"

She looked startled.

"Yes, but not recently. Anyone on this estate who's got any sense doesn't talk about him. He's an evil man, Detective. Emily knew him way back, before his career in killing people got off the ground. He used to live around here. But she hadn't seen or heard from him in years."

"Were they close?"

"No. They were both in a group of teenagers who went around together. There was Emily, Ken, who she later married, a few others, plus Vinny and Carol."

"You're sure he didn't contact her recently? Not even a phone call?"

"Not as far as I know," she replied. "If he had, I'm sure Emily would have told me."

"Does Ricky know that his mum knew Costello?"

"Heavens no, and neither does anyone else. Everyone who was part of that group has moved on."

"Was Emily happy at work?"

"Yes. It wasn't the most exciting job but it paid the bills. They are a friendly bunch and that helped."

"Jet Holdings. Do you know who they are?"

"No, I've never heard of them."

Rocco noted a slight wobble in her voice as she answered that one. "Do you know where Emily was going on Tuesday? She was dressed up, hair and make-up perfect. Was she meeting someone?"

"I honestly don't know. If she was, she didn't tell me."

Rocco believed her.

"You mentioned a 'Carol.' Who was she?"

"I don't remember her full name. But she doesn't live around here anymore."

* * *

"Guv!" Imogen called out as Calladine returned to the incident room. "The post-mortem on Emily Blackwell has turned up something important. The bullets that killed Emily and bust Davey's legs were fired from the same gun."

Calladine peered over Imogen's shoulder at the computer screen. She was right. Roxy Atkins's report was pretty clear. So there was a link between Emily and Davey — had to be. But what was it? Calladine was stumped. He couldn't imagine what they'd have in common. But there was Emily's son, Ricky. He knew Davey. Had he got something to do with this?

"Anyone have any ideas? A supposedly clean-living woman and the likes of Wayne Davey. Who had they both upset?"

Rocco came into the office. "I've got something new on the Costello angle. Enid Mason confirmed that Emily and he did know each other. When they were teenagers they went around together with some others from the estate. Ken Blackwell too. But Ken's doing time in Strangeways. Her work was fine and I drew another blank with Jet Holdings. Although I think she was lying."

Calladine went to the incident board and drew a line linking the two names, Emily and Costello. "Any recent contact?"

"Enid says not."

"Should we tell DCI King?" Rocco asked.

Calladine nodded towards the closed office door. "It wouldn't surprise me if she didn't already know. She might let us in at some point."

"The PM report also stated that Emily had been killed at Clough Bottom," Imogen continued. "She'd been beaten. Her legs were broken. The pathologist said they were hit with something long and hard, like a bat. She was hit on the head, fell forward and then was shot in the back. Roxy Atkins is looking at her clothing. It might shed some light on who laid her out like that. Costello might have contacted Emily recently," she suggested.

"For what reason? To lure her up to Clough Bottom and kill her? The fact they were pally once isn't motive enough. Emily led a perfectly ordinary life. She wasn't involved in drugs or crime of any sort and neither was her son. She'd be of no interest to Costello."

"Something from the past perhaps?"

"See what you can dig up, Imogen. If you don't get anywhere I think it's time we spoke to the man himself. Did we request an interview with Costello?"

"I rang his assistant, Gavin Trent. Smooth and sneaky if you ask me," Imogen told the team. "He confirmed that it was a company car and said he'd check who had booked it out. He's promised to get back soon as."

"Keep on his back. It'll be interesting to see how they wriggle out of this one. Keep at it with Emily's past. Find out about that money she was paid each month. Also dig up what you can about Ricky Blackwell. He was being bullied. Try and find out what that was all about. Is he in a gang? Is he mixed up in the drug dealing on that estate? That sort of thing. I can't imagine that Ricky has attracted Costello's attention but we'll look at it to make sure."

"That woman at the auction, sir. She's still a bit of a mystery. The auctioneer doesn't know anything about her. She registered to bid and gave her address as the Pennine Inn. It's that hotel out Hopecross way, which means she's not local. The auctioneer told me that the cottage was advertised widely. But I was there, and apart from her the only people interested were local."

"Okay, I'll take that. I'll go up there and see what she has to say — if she's still there. You saw her, Imogen. What sort of woman am I looking for?"

"Definitely upmarket. She wore good clothes. She had a slight American accent and was very attractive with shoulder-length dark hair."

"Should be easy to spot, then."

"She certainly drew all eyes at the auction. She even had Julian staring."

* * *

"Calladine!" DCI Rhona Birch called as he was on his way out. "A discreet word if you've got a minute."

He followed her into her office and sat down.

"Has DCI King shared anything with you?"

"No, ma'am. But she gave me the impression that things aren't going her way. It's nothing she's said, just stuff she's asked me and her reactions to the answers."

"I've just had an interesting phone conversation. I'm not sure what to make of it. The caller asked for the SIO on the shooting of the boy." She waved her hand dismissively. "As far as I'm concerned, that's you. DCI King is officially here because of the Emily Blackwell murder."

Except that they both knew she wasn't.

"Plus I was unaware until a conversation with McCabe this morning that she is in fact a DI. Currently she is *acting* DCI due to Greco being on leave." She regarded Calladine for a moment. "You got off lightly. Ordinarily it would be him you'd be dealing with. So despite her attitude, count yourself lucky."

Calladine weighed this little nugget in his head. Eliza King or Greco. What was the job trying to do to him?

"What about this caller, ma'am?"

"A member of your team contacted a Gavin Trent. The caller suggested that you speak to her instead. She is one of Costello's people. But she was a little vague as to her exact role."

"Does she want me to ring her?"

"No, that's the thing that bothers me. She's here in Leesworth. She has been for a day or two. We can't dismiss the fact that all the problems we've had started with her arrival."

"A woman, you say, and on Costello's payroll. It is possible. But it's still the same old question — why? What does Costello want? What excuse does she have for being here?"

"She intends to discuss that with you. Mr Trent has asked her to speak candidly about the limo on the Hobfield yesterday."

"Did she give her name?"

"Tanya Mallon. Mean anything to you?"

"A Mrs Mallon was at the auction of Clough Cottage yesterday. It's probably the same woman. Is she coming in?"

"No. She has suggested you meet for lunch at the Pennine Inn. She's staying there. I said you would be willing to listen to what she has to say. Did I do right?"

Calladine nodded. "I was just about to go and speak to her. I'm presuming she viewed the cottage prior to the auction, in which case she might have seen something."

"Tread carefully. Find out what she's doing here but don't antagonise her. Tanya Mallon is on Costello's payroll and the man's a killer. Be pleasant and listen to her. Weigh up what she has to say and report back. But keep this to yourself for now."

"We're not sharing this information with DCI King?"

"Does she share anything with us?"

"Fair comment."

"We don't want her getting overexcited, do we?"

Chapter 9

"Mrs Hunter?" Annie Naden smiled at the woman who opened the door. "I wonder if you can help me."

The woman scowled.

"I believe you've lived in this house for a long time."

"Nigh on fifty years," she replied. "What's it got to do with you?"

"It's about an ex-neighbour of yours. Me and my husband have bought Clough Cottage up on the hill and we've found something that belonged to one of them."

"That dump! Hope you've got money behind you."

Annie Naden wanted this woman to talk to her, otherwise she wouldn't have given her the time of day. She'd perfected her rudeness down to the last grimace. "We found a school satchel. There was a name and address in one of the books. They used to live next door to you."

Another doubtful scowl. "Who were these neighbours?"

"The Rhodes family. Does that name ring any bells?"

"Rhodes." She virtually spat the name. "Yes, I remember them. He was a drinker and she worked at the mill up there." She pointed towards the town. "It's gone now, the paper mill. Pulled it down and threw up a supermarket and some houses."

"Did they have a daughter called Carol?"

"Yes. Given the stock she came from, a surprisingly nice girl. There was a son as well, as far as I remember. Don't know what happened to him."

"That's great. Do you know where Carol Rhodes is now?"

Mrs Hunter stared at Annie. Her eyes narrowed. "Are you trying to be funny, lass?"

"No, not at all," Annie replied. "I'd really like to give the satchel back to her, that's all."

"Well, you'll have a job, love. Carol Rhodes walked out of her parents' house some forty years ago and no one's seen her since."

* * *

The Pennine Inn was situated along a narrow country lane above the village of Hopecross. From here on a clear day you could see right over the valley, across the village of Lowermill to Leesdon beyond.

The restaurant was surprisingly busy for such a remote location. Calladine cast his dark eyes around the diners. A woman waved. He wondered how she'd recognised him.

"DI Calladine?" she drawled in the American accent Imogen had mentioned. "Good of you to come at such short notice."

"Mrs Mallon?"

The woman nodded.

Imogen was right about the woman being attractive. He guessed she was about his own age but she carried it much better. She looked as if she was throwing everything she'd got at the aging process and winning. Frequent visits to the salon had paid off. She had glossy hair and her make-up and clothes were immaculate. Everything faultless. Plastic surgery? he wondered, looking at her perfectly formed nose, flawless skin and full lips. He mustn't get sidetracked. This woman had an agenda. He mustn't forget that despite the looks, she was still one of Costello's minions.

She'd reserved them a table by a large picture window that looked out over the valley.

She smiled. "This hotel is in a beautiful spot. The countryside around here is amazing."

"So you work for Vinny Costello?" He wasn't in the mood for polite conversation.

"Occasionally I do," she allowed. Her brown eyes twinkled with amusement. "But not exclusively for him. I came to Leesworth more as a favour than anything else. He used to live around here, you know."

"Yes I do know, but that was a long time ago. What puzzles me is why he's interested in the place now."

"Here." She passed him a menu. "Let's order lunch. They do fabulous food here. Order whatever you fancy, it's on Rose Argent Enterprises."

The charm offensive was gathering pace.

Calladine placed the menu back on the table. "What does Costello want from Leesdon?"

She gave him a little smile. "You must try not to be so suspicious, Inspector. Mr Costello has a past, as I'm sure you know, but there is another side to him."

"You mean apart from the kill first and sod the consequences side," he replied, parodying her smile.

"You're a policeman. You're bound to be sceptical, it would be unnatural if you weren't."

"So go on, indulge me. Why are you here?"

"Memories, Inspector. That's what this is all about."

Not so much as a flicker on that lovely face. She seemed to mean it. She had either made lying into an art form or it was the truth. "Now I am intrigued. You are suggesting that Costello has turned into a sentimental old man. I'm not having that. There has to be more."

"No, that's it, pure and simple. Mr Costello asked me to come here, visit specific places and take photos. An easy enough task, but I appear to have attracted your attention."

"You were on the Hobfield yesterday when a young man was shot."

"I believe so. Although I must say at once that I didn't see anything." She looked perturbed. "I didn't stay long." She rummaged in her handbag and took out a camera. "This is what I was doing, Inspector." She showed him the images. There were about twenty of them, all different views of the Hobfield. "I've also taken a few of local landmarks and the surrounding countryside."

"Why? Why would Costello want this little lot?"

She put the camera back. "I have no idea, but he does. I didn't ask questions. I'm getting very well paid, so I did as he asked. Photos he wants, so that's what he'll get."

"Did he specify what you should photograph?"

She smiled. "Not really. Apart from the Hobfield it's up to me. A montage of Leesworth — warts and all."

"Did he ask you to look anyone up? Old friends for example?"

"No, he didn't mention anyone."

"A woman Costello might have known from the old days was murdered near Clough Cottage. The cottage is on a hillside known locally as Clough Bottom."

"I hope you're not thinking that that has anything to do with me, Inspector. I can assure you I'm not in the habit of killing people." She spoke with feeling. "Who was she?"

"Emily Blackwell. Costello will have known her as Emily Mason."

"Sorry, the name means nothing to me."

"I saw your limo pull up on the estate yesterday. You must have seen me and my colleague."

"I don't remember. There were people about but I didn't take much notice. Like I told you, I was there to photograph the tower blocks."

"Did you get out of the car?"

"Briefly. For a few seconds, that's all. After that I left and drove round to the common and took a few snaps there."

"You show an interest in the cottage and a woman is killed. You visit the Hobfield within minutes of a particularly nasty shooting. I'd say you were bad luck, Mrs Mallon."

"Sheer coincidence, Inspector. There would have been lots of people tramping round that cottage because of the auction, and the Hobfield is hardly whiter than white, is it?"

"Anywhere else around here that Costello wanted photographing?"

"No. Like I said, he left it up to me. There is nothing untoward going on. You really must stop seeing the criminal in everybody."

"That's a big ask where Costello's concerned."

Her smile became a pout. "He isn't like you think. He can be charming and generous. I was wary too when I first met him. I'm not stupid. I'd heard rumours about his reputation, but I decided to make up my own mind. He's never put a foot wrong when we've been together."

"So he reeled you in. You're not having an affair with the man, are you?"

"No. Business only, Inspector. Costello has a wife and grown-up kids. He is very happy with what he has."

"What were you doing at the auction yesterday morning?"

Her perfectly made-up eyes raked over his face. What was she thinking? Perhaps she was wondering how he knew about her bid.

"I was curious," she replied.

She was lying. There was a slight flush on her cheeks. The words caught in her throat. It was enough.

"It's a property with potential," she said.

"You got that straight from the brochure. It's old, practically derelict and needs a shedload of money spending on it. So, come on, what's the real reason?"

She smiled again. "You're right. It was a stupid idea. I realise that now. I saw it on a poster in the auction house window as I passed. It looked so romantic, situated on the hillside like that. I decided to go along." She paused for a moment, delving in her handbag. "The brochure . . . don't you find the description tempting?"

"You went along intending to buy. You bid on the place, so I heard. So what happened?"

The expression on her face hardened. "I saw sense. The place is falling down. A couple of men, builders, were talking and I overheard what they said. It put me off. I got a call from a client and used it as an excuse to duck out. Rude of me I know, but no harm was done."

"So you went up there — to Clough Cottage?"

"Yes, a brief visit. It was nothing like the romantic image painted in the brochure. But it had a certain charm. If I could have got the place cheap, then fair enough, but that wasn't going to happen."

"Did Costello know what you were doing?"

She shook her head. "I saw no reason to tell him."

"When are you planning to leave?"

"Not yet. Perhaps the end of the week."

"Can I ask what's keeping you in Leesworth?"

"I've a few more photos to take and I plan to do some shopping in Manchester."

Calladine was considering this when his mobile rang. It was DCI Birch from the station.

"Wayne Davey is dead."

Stark and to the point.

"From his injuries?"

"Nothing so simple. He was stabbed early this morning while he lay in his hospital bed unable to defend himself. Did you speak to him?"

"No. He was still out of it when I enquired."

"Why wasn't he being watched?"

"He was. The uniform must have been having a break."

She let that go, thankfully.

"What I don't understand is why. It doesn't make sense. He could easily have been killed at the scene yesterday. Why wait until he was hospitalised then stab him?"

Calladine got up and walked towards the main door. He didn't want Tanya Mallon overhearing. "Perhaps because whoever did his legs wanted to warn him. It was a gesture. Someone else killed him."

There was silence. Birch was taking a few seconds to consider that one.

"It still doesn't add up, Calladine. Davey was a nobody, a face from the Hobfield. Who had he upset?"

"Perhaps we should take that one to DCI King. What's she doing this morning anyway?"

"I've no idea. She's closeted in your office on her laptop. The quieter she stays the better if you ask me."

"Could the hospital give us anything?"

"The nurse who was attending to Davey says he had no visitors. The only people on the ward this morning were hospital staff. But there was a porter. He was supposed to take a patient to X-ray and that never happened. She can't give a description. They all wear a uniform and look the same, according to her."

"Any CCTV?"

"DI Rockliffe is looking through it now."

"I'm still with Tanya Mallon. She's charming but not much help. She's doing her best to convince me that Costello sent her on a nostalgia trip. But I don't believe it. We need to find Archer and Garrett. The fact that they are missing is worrying. I'll finish up here and come in. Would you tell uniform that both those young men are officially missing? We could do with photos of them both from the families."

"DCI King?"

"She knows more than she's saying."

"It might help if I had a word."

"Best of luck with that one, ma'am."

* * *

"What do you reckon happened to her?" Annie Naden asked her husband. He was plastering the ceiling in the sitting room and not in the mood for discussing Annie's latest obsession.

"Well, she did one, didn't she?"

"But why would she?"

"You said she was pregnant. Things were different for girls back then. She most likely went to live with a relative in another town then got a job," said Jack. He waved at the room. "You need to let this go, we've got a load of work to do. Helping me is what you should be doing, Annie. Not chasing ghosts from the past."

"I can't help it. Carol has got to me. It's weird, I know, given I never knew her, but I want to find out what happened."

"Like I said, she'll have done one."

"That's not what Mrs Hunter said. She made out that Carol disappeared. That is a whole lot more sinister than simply getting a job in another town. If that was what had happened then her family would have told folk. She'd have come back — visited."

"My advice is, don't get involved. That thing is old. It's filthy. You should get rid. Sling it in the bin and forget you ever found it."

"Carol Rhodes was only fifteen years old, Jack! Girls of that age don't just wander off and disappear."

"It was forty years ago. Mrs Hunter won't have remembered it right. It's been too long."

"I'm going to find someone else. Carol must have had family in this town."

"Not that my parents are aware of. But they do remember who lived here. A Mary Slater and her daughter rented the place for a while. They did a disappearing act too. Probably couldn't pay the rent. Don't get carried away, Annie. It's only a school satchel we've found, not the Crown Jewels."

"That's not the point. I can't get the girl out of my mind. She had plans, Jack. Her diary was in that bag. The last entry she made said that she was pregnant. Did she have the baby? What did she do with it? Perhaps something happened to them both."

"Don't dramatize this. There will be an explanation."

Annie didn't doubt it. The problem was, her imagination had come up with so many. She decided to have another word with Mrs Hunter. If nothing else she'd probably know Carol's extended family.

"My dad's bringing the water people round tomorrow. They'll inspect the well and draw up plans for what we need to do." He looked at his wife. "It's going to cost a bit. Dad says we'll need new pipework and a filter system. It might set us back a bit."

But Annie wasn't listening. She was getting ready to go out.

* * *

Jack was right. She should be back at the cottage helping out. But she couldn't get the mystery of Carol Rhodes out of her head. A few more questions, another chat with Mrs Hunter and then she'd drop it.

Annie didn't fancy knocking on that door again. The woman wasn't the friendliest. But what choice did she have? The other people around there were too young to have known the Rhodes family.

"I've already told you, no one's seen the girl in years." The woman spoke as soon as she saw Annie on her doorstep again. She accompanied the words with a look geared to discourage any further questions.

"You've had time to think. Perhaps you've thought of something, or someone else, who could help me. Surely people must have wondered what happened to Carol?"

Mrs Hunter shook her head. "More than likely, but I can't help. Most folk around here didn't get on with that family. They were a bad lot, particularly him. I doubt they gave a damn what happened to the girl. She's well out of it if you ask me."

"I think she was pregnant when she disappeared."

Mrs Hunter gave her a quizzical look. "You sure?"

"Well, it's in her diary. I found it in the satchel. She was only fifteen. She must have told her family."

"She'd have got rid more like. Clough Cottage you said? That was Mary Slater's place." She gave Annie a knowing nod. "There's your answer."

"What do you mean?"

"Back then girls in this town tramped up that hill to see Mary Slater all the time. Unwanted pregnancies were her speciality, if you get my point."

Annie stared at the woman. "She did abortions?"

"You didn't get that from me. But if something went wrong, the doctor's surgery might have a record."

"Problem is they wouldn't tell me even if they have," Annie replied. "Are her family still around here?"

"Sorry, love, I've no idea. I've not seen any of them for years."

"So you can't think of anyone who can help me?"

"The police might. They investigated when she went missing."

Annie shot her a look. "Why didn't you say so before? The satchel could be evidence."

"I doubt it. They decided she'd done a bunk with that lad of hers. A real bad lot off the Hobfield. Vinny Costello was his name."

Chapter 10

Back at the station Calladine rang the Duggan and asked to speak to Julian Batho.

"Emily Blackwell. She was brought in yesterday from Clough Bottom. It looks highly likely that the body had been tampered with after death. I know Roxy is looking. Has anything turned up yet?"

"Doctor Bower did the PM. He's noted your concerns in the report. It looks as if her clothing had been rearranged and make-up applied — plus something about the shoes. From the soil on her feet it is thought she walked barefoot up the hill. We have retrieved a set of fingerprints from them and they are not those of the deceased."

"So someone put them back on."

"Looks like it. The shoes were black patent," he told Calladine. "Good and shiny, the marks are clear. However there is no match on record. So, find me a suspect and we might be in business."

"The people we've been dealing with so far, Archer and his mates, all have records. Not one of them, then."

"No. Doctor Atkins is having the lipstick analysed. She tells me it's an expensive brand. That fact might lead somewhere."

"Bad luck about the cottage by the way," said Calladine.

"Frankly I think it was just as well. Imogen has quite the wrong idea about the extent of my capabilities. They do not run to patching up brickwork or laying down floors. Whoever buys that dump will have to part with a king's ransom to put it right."

"I suggested she speak to Zoe."

"We did. We're going to look at a semi in Lowermill at the weekend, after the christening."

"Hope it suits."

"Keep it under wraps for the time being. I haven't told her yet. We have a conflict over what type of property to buy. You know her, she's the out-in-the-sticks type. I'm afraid I'm a little more conservative."

"If you get something on the body I'll be here or on my mobile."

He didn't fancy a long talk about Imogen's dream home. "When are you doing the PM on Wayne Davey?"

"Later today. If I get anything interesting you'll be the first to know. The same gun was used in both shootings," Julian told him. "Interesting, don't you think?"

"I wish I knew what it meant. We have a gunman. He's on our patch and he's used the thing twice. Problem is, we don't know who he is or what he's after. Now we have a stabbing too."

"I'm checking the database. It's unlikely the gun is new. If it's been used in the past, it might help to know where."

"Thanks, Julian."

Calladine's mobile showed a text from Ruth. She wanted him to meet her at the church later that day to go over the procedures for the christening with the vicar. He hadn't told Eve yet. He decided to ring her.

Only the main participants were required for the rehearsal but Eve Buckley had come along anyway.

"I hope Ruth doesn't mind. I took this as an opportunity. I see so very little of you," she chided. "You need to call round more. I want you in our lives, Tom. I'm getting sick of saying it."

"It's work that keeps me away," he lied. "Long days, long nights, and hardly a moment to spare. We've got a hard one on at the moment."

"You'd tell me anything, you would. You eat, don't you? You should come and eat with us."

It wasn't that easy. Eve Buckley might be his mother but she was still a stranger. And socially they were miles apart. She was a darling of the Leesworth elite, a golf club member and all the other stuff Calladine didn't go in for. He'd been to one do at hers. On that occasion he'd met his uncle and discovered he was the chief super.

"It was nice of you to ask me to accompany you to the christening," she said. "I appreciate the thought."

It had been Ruth's idea, actually. He shuffled uncomfortably.

"Who's to be godmother?"

Another problem. Ruth had asked his ex, Monika. Ruth Bayliss was pulling out all the stops to make this a right tricky one for him. He wasn't daft. Having Eve as his plus-one meant the path was clear for Monika.

"Any others on your team got roles?"

"No, Eve. Just me. They'll be here for the actual event though. Until then it's work all the way, I'm afraid."

"How's that nice couple, the detective and the professor?"

"Still being nice — well to each other anyway." He smiled. "They're looking for a house to buy. They just missed one at the auction — Clough Cottage."

Eve grimaced. "That awful place! They should count themselves lucky. It's got a bad history."

"Why? What's wrong with it? Seriously detached, no near neighbours, make as much noise as you want. Perhaps I should have had a go myself."

"Clough Cottage has a dreadful past," she confided. "It's full of ghosts and believe me, Tom, they're not happy ones."

"First I've heard."

"You're probably too young."

"Go on then — spill. Tell me the gory details."

"It's not funny, really. It's a tragic tale. A woman called Mary Slater used to live there. She was the person the girls went to if they got themselves into trouble . . ." She pulled a face. "You know."

Calladine shook his head. He'd had no idea.

"Surely you must have heard something about her, and that cottage? There's not much you don't know about this town."

"Whatever it is, it must have gone right over my head. And what do you mean, girls in trouble?"

"I'm talking about young, unmarried girls who'd got themselves pregnant. More often than not they were on their own. The bloke who'd got them that way did a runner. Mary Slater fixed things. She carried out illegal abortions, Tom. *Granny Slater* we used to call her, though God knows why. She had no grandchildren, just that little girl of hers."

"That's why I wouldn't know. Abortion only became legal after 1967. Before that I was too young."

Eve huffed. "Perhaps I shouldn't be saying this, but even after 1967 abortions were still hard to get in some places, Leesdon in particular. We had a GP who was dead set against it. He was in his sixties and very old-fashioned. He was here until seventy-two when his brother took over. He was no better."

"Couldn't the girls insist? Attitudes had changed by the seventies. Couldn't they ask to be referred to a different doctor?"

"They could try, but it was never going to happen. Medically, Leesdon was a backwater. The doctor would delay. He'd cancel the girl's appointments. The nurse at the practice did exactly as he told her. In the end it was easier to walk up that hill and see Granny Slater."

"When did she leave Clough Cottage?"

"I've no idea, but there was a bit of a mystery as I recall. In the end it was presumed she did a runner to avoid paying the rent."

"And no one's seen her since?"

"I wouldn't know, Tom. She wasn't popular. When Mary Slater ventured down to Leesdon for shopping, folk had been known to spit in her face."

He looked at her. He'd only discovered recently that Eve was his birth mother. She'd been pregnant in her teens with no husband. The man she'd been seeing — his father, Frank Calladine, had a wife at home. "Did you ever consider . . . ?"

The question hung in the air between them. Her eyes dropped to the floor. "Yes, Tom, I did. At one point I even discussed it with your dad. It was a way out for both of us. I didn't want to raise a child and he wouldn't leave Freda, not even for me."

"But you didn't go through with it. You must have changed your mind."

"I was never keen and Frank wouldn't hear of it. He'd already made up his mind anyway to take you himself, and the rest you know."

"The vicar wants us inside now!" Ruth called to them.

"We'd better go." Eve took his arm. "Who's that woman? She keeps looking at you." She nodded towards Monika.

"An old friend of Ruth's and mine. She's the godmother."

"Do you know her?"

"Yes. Monika and I have history, and not all good."

"Why not go and speak to her?"

"That could be tricky. She doesn't like me very much."

Eve slapped his arm. "Don't be so soft. She's interested, a woman can tell."

Eve deliberately walked away to join the others as they went inside the church. Monika was hanging back. Waiting for him?

She smiled thinly. "It's been a while. Can I suggest we just get on with this without too much fuss? We both know what this is about. It's Ruth having a go at relationship first aid."

"I don't mind, if you don't," Calladine replied. "Besides, it's nice to see you. You look well."

She did too. Monika had lost weight and her hair was different, a bit longer and curly. It suited her.

"You look bloody awful. What happened?" Blunt as ever.

"The job, no Ruth because of the baby, a stroppy DCI to deal with . . . stuff happens, you know that."

"I know how you are. Have a night off, a weekend away. You should consider it, Tom, before your body steps in and lets you down."

"I'm thinking of going to the gym."

"Gym. Huh. It'll take more than that. A complete change of lifestyle is called for, Tom Calladine." She slapped his belly with the back of her hand. "And your hair! Why all the grey?"

He shrugged. "Age, I suppose. I do my best."

"You do nothing. You need taking in hand."

"You are a hard woman, Monika."

"That woman you're with. She's a Buckley, isn't she?"

"Yep. That's Eve Buckley. Turns out she's my birth mother."

"Birth mother? What on earth are you talking about?"

"It was in the box Freda left me — the one you had in safekeeping."

Monika was the manageress of the care home Freda, his mother, had lived in for the last months of her life.

Monika stared at him. "Are you being serious?"

"Straight up. She is the big secret my dad kept for years."

"Eve Buckley — instant mother. Who'd have thought it?" She looked at him again. "You're not having me on, are you?"

"No! She really is my mother. Believe me, I was just as surprised when I found out."

"Your dad had an affair and Freda never knew?"

"That's about the size of it. Freda took me on and never said anything. She must have wanted me to know the truth though. Hence the box with my past in it."

"You've landed on your feet in that case. The Buckleys are loaded."

"She's got two other kids, so I imagine I'm well down the pecking order."

"Eve Buckley never approached you in all these years?"

"No. Apparently it was agreed between the three of them that she'd not interfere. I'd still be oblivious now if it wasn't for Freda's letter."

"And you're bringing her to the christening instead of the glamorous reporter?"

She didn't know. He'd have to tell her. Talking about Lydia always hurt. "Lydia was murdered," he said quietly. "Fallon had her shot."

They were walking towards the church, but this made Monika stop dead in her tracks. "I'd no idea."

"Like me, she was scheduled to give evidence against him. Fallon wanted us both dead but he went for Lydia first." Despite the fact they'd split up before it had happened, it was painful to talk about Lydia. Particularly about the way she'd died. "He's dead himself now. Evil bastard."

Monika put her hand on his arm. "I'm sorry, Tom. You've had a lot to cope with."

"So now you understand why I look like I do," he joked.

"It might help to talk. If you want to come round and have a meal one night, ring me. We'll have a catch up."

Calladine smiled at her. He might just do that.

The practice didn't last long. Harry Ireson was exercising his lungs again and Ruth was at the end of her tether.

"Why won't he stop?" she hissed at Calladine. "It's bloody embarrassing."

"Give him here," he offered. "I'll walk him round the graveyard, check on my parents."

"Great. Now he'll have nightmares as well."

With the infant in his arms he walked out into the last of the evening sunshine. His parents were in a plot behind the church.

"Want me to come with you?" Eve asked.

"If you want to. I'm really just trying to get this one off. Give Ruth a break."

They found his parents' grave.

"I loved him, you know. Frank Calladine," Eve said

"He died before I could really get to know him. All I remember was him always going on at me about something. Not keeping my stuff tidy, being hopeless at school, and looking like an urchin. I always felt like a disappointment."

"He loved you. He was your dad, that's what they're like." Eve was holding a red rose, taken from a bush in the hedgerow. She laid it on the grave. "You keep it nice."

"Actually it's not me. There's a bloke who does odd jobs for the vicar. He looks after things for a fee."

"The work leave you no time?"

"Never enough."

He saw Monika walking towards them.

"Tom!" she called over to him.

"Look, I'll leave you to talk to your friend. See you Sunday if not before." Eve kissed his cheek and left.

Monika was laughing at him. "Suits you, a babe in your arms."

"I'm not bad at it either. See — he's sleeping."

She linked his arm. "Your parents . . . I was fond of Freda. She was straight-talking and no trouble, even at the end." She nodded at the grave. "It's nice, but bare. You should plant something — a couple of rose bushes," she said, looking at Eve's single red rose. "Freda would like that."

"I should pay more attention. Do stuff myself. Okay. I'll get something from the garden centre this weekend."

"I can come with you if you like. Help you choose."

That wasn't a bad idea. "We could lunch in that pub you always liked on the way back," he suggested.

"Okay. I'd like that."

There was something about Monika that Calladine had always found comforting. Being with her was easy. He could just be himself.

Monika pointed to another grave on the way out. "That one has always intrigued me . . ."

"I'll take him," Ruth interrupted, coming up behind them.

Calladine handed him back. "He's dropped off."

". . . She hadn't a soul in the world yet the grave is pristine and there are always fresh flowers left every week."

Ruth shuddered. "That's weird, Monika. It must be a relative. Maybe it was a long-lost someone who inherited money from her."

"There was no one that I can remember. She was a jolly soul though, one of my favourites. Old Mrs Jackson spent the last three years of her life with me."

"I could do with taking you home with me, Tom," Ruth said. "It seems I just have to put this one within a few feet of you and he falls asleep. I wish I had that power!"

"He'll settle down."

"D'you promise? At this rate I'll never get back to work."

"Perhaps work could come to you. I'll come round to yours tomorrow sometime, run a few things past you. The case could do with some fresh input."

"Make sure you do. I've got serious withdrawal symptoms."

* * *

Mick Garrett yelped in pain. The last kick in the ribs had winded him. He was lying on the ground by the riverbank, on his side with his hands and ankles taped behind his back.

"That mate of yours gone and left you?" the man sneered, kicking him again.

Garrett was gasping for breath. "No idea. I saw him a few hours ago but now he's dropped out of sight."

The man landed another vicious kick, this time in Garrett's guts. It made the lad want to throw up. "Leave off," he rasped. "I know nowt. If I did, I'd tell you."

"You're lying. What're you doing here tonight? The pair of you are up to something, aren't you?"

The man was kneeling beside him, his face so close Garrett could feel the warm breath on his forehead.

"No. I saw him earlier. I followed him here." Garrett's breathing was laboured. His ribs hurt like hell. The bastard must have broken a couple.

"Archer is doing a job for me. I wasn't sure if I could trust him. Now I know I can't." The man was tapping on his mobile again. "He doesn't answer. Why? Where has he gone?"

"He's scared. He thinks whoever did Wayne Davey, will come after us. He'll lie low for a bit, that's all," Garrett said.

"Did he say who was after him?" The man grabbed a handful of Garrett's hair and slammed his face into the mud.

Garrett screamed in pain. His nose had caught a large stone. "Let off, mate. I can't help you."

In response, the man slammed his head into the ground again.

"The bloke heading up the rival firm to Costello. He said there was a battle going on for the estate and we should keep our heads down."

"Stupid fool. He'd no right to say anything. He should learn to keep his mouth shut."

Garrett had no idea who this man was. He'd never seen him before. He'd known his mate was waiting for someone so he'd hung around. A bad mistake. He should have laid low like Archer had told him to. Why hadn't his mate said the bloke was bloody dangerous?

"Do you work for Costello?" Garrett groaned.

The man laughed humourlessly. "No, son. I work for myself." He was on his mobile again. "Where would he go to ground?"

"The flat. That's where we've both been holed up."

"Well, he's not there now. The police are all over it. Somewhere else. Come on, you must know."

"You've lost me." Garrett spat out a gob of blood. The blow on his head had made his nose bleed.

"I'm running out of patience. If you have anything to offer you'd better speak up now."

Garrett shook his head. "I could look for him for you," he suggested. "The lads on the estate, they'd talk to me."

"Not an option. No information, so no use." He knelt down beside Garrett. "Pity. In different circumstances I could have used you." He took a knife from his pocket and placed it against Garrett's throat.

The lad screamed, "No!" He felt the cold steel against his neck. "I can help! I'll do anything."

"It's just business, nothing personal," said the man.

Garrett struggled but it was hopeless. The man put a hand around his throat and squeezed. At the same time the blade went in smooth and deep between two ribs. It pierced the chest wall and entered the heart. As he took his final breath the man kicked him down the embankment and into the black waters of the river.

* * *

The dog had gotten used to his evening stroll. Calladine usually took him to the common, let him run loose for five minutes or so, and headed home. Given all the health advice he was getting perhaps it was time to extend the walk a little further. Sam seemed up for it.

He'd taken the transition from Marilyn to Calladine well. Unlike Marilyn, the DI didn't treat him like an infant. He spoke to the dog as if he was one of his team, a member who didn't answer back. Tonight he walked around the perimeter of the common and onto the lane that ran the back way to Hopecross. "We'll have a hike up this hill. Head-clearing exercise." He patted the dog.

There was little traffic so Sam ran free. He stuck to the pavement and didn't stray far from Calladine's heels. Calladine hadn't realised that once you reached the highest point of the lane, you could see the Pennine Inn. There was a pull-in for cars and a bright red sports job was parked up.

A woman was standing against the bonnet with a pair of binoculars pressed to her eyes. Sam barked and ran towards her. She jumped.

"Sorry."

"You should have him on a lead," she said, brushing at her dress. "He's moulting. But he's a lovely boy." She bent down and ruffled Sam around the ears. "I forgive you, handsome," she added, and plonked a kiss on his head.

What was it with women and dogs?

"Something interesting caught your eye?" She didn't look the birdwatching type but according to Ruth this was the place to see hawks.

"A moonlighting employee. It's not allowed. There can be safety issues. I knew Annette was up to something. Telling me she couldn't work tonight because of a family problem. She must think I'm stupid. I saw the note in the book."

He nodded at the hotel. "That's an expensive place."

"The bloke Annette is in there with is a regular. That's good business I'm losing. She'd better have a good excuse or I'll sack her."

Calladine coughed. He'd no idea what she was on about. "Do you live locally?"

"Sort of. Droylsden. Know it?"

"That's on the way to Manchester. I've probably passed through it a couple of times."

"She's come out here thinking I won't find out. This is way off the beaten track."

He chuckled. "You're not dressed for climbing hills either."

She smiled back. "I'm a city girl. I should explain. I run a model and escort agency. Annette is one of my girls. Or was one of my girls until she branched out on her own." She took a card from her bag.

It was bright red with a picture of a glamourous woman on it. She watched him with a smirk on her face.

"I see no point in flowering it up. I supply escorts for bored businessmen. You know the type, away from home, needing a dinner partner or a little company."

Well, that sounded a bit dodgy, but she wasn't the least embarrassed to talk about her work to a complete stranger. He gave her a quizzical look. Should he tell her he was police in case she said something out of turn? Calladine was curious. Many so-called escort agencies were nothing but a cover for something more dubious. Was that her game? He decided to leave it. She was open and honest and he liked that. Funny that. How you could be drawn to certain people without having to know anything about them. She was nice-looking too. She had black hair falling just below her chin, cut into a swingy bob shape with a full fringe. She wore bright red lipstick. Red, it seemed, was her colour. Her curvy figure was wrapped in a deep red and black dress that clung and there were red sling-back high heels on her feet.

He held out his hand. "Tom Calladine. And this is Sam."

"Shelley Mortimer, but friends call me Shez," she replied, taking his hand and squeezing lightly. "Fancy a drink?"

"Not over there if you don't mind."

"God no. I was thinking about that dive in the town down there: the Wheatsheaf."

That was more like it. He nodded at her.

"In that case let's go get hammered, Tom Calladine."

Chapter 11

Thursday

Rocco knocked on Enid Mason's door. No answer.
Despite their conversation the day before, Rocco wanted
to clarify a couple of points.

"They've gone off somewhere, mate," a voice called
from along the deck.

"What do you mean?"

"This morning. Suitcases and all. They got a taxi and
left."

"Did you see which taxi firm?"

"Staples, at the end of the estate."

Hopefully they'd have a record. Rocco started down
the stairs. The place was quiet. Even the square was empty.
The shooting had rattled folk and who could blame them?
But he couldn't understand why Enid and Ricky would do
a runner like this. What was it they were afraid of? Rocco
went over yesterday's conversation with Enid. Something
he'd asked must have spooked her.

Staples Taxis was a father and son business. Rocco walked into the office and showed his badge to the young man behind the counter.

"One of your drivers picked up a fare from Heron House this morning — Enid Mason and her nephew. I need to know where they were going."

"You're in luck. I know them and that was me." He flicked through a notebook. "I took them to the coach station in Manchester, Chorlton Street."

"You don't know where they were going?"

"No. Neither of them said more than a couple of words for the entire journey. Weird if you ask me. They had luggage. I presumed they were going away on holiday. But they couldn't even raise a smile."

Back outside, Rocco rang the nick and spoke to Imogen. "Enid Mason has done a runner and taken Ricky with her. I'm coming back to the nick now. In the meantime would you check with the coach company and see if you can find out where they've gone?"

Rocco couldn't think of anything in the conversation yesterday that would have caused this reaction. Enid had answered his questions openly. But the fact they'd left had to be down to him, and that was annoying.

* * *

"They got a coach to Cardiff," Imogen told Rocco as he walked through the office door.

"Why would they run? Who do they know in Cardiff?" Calladine was sitting at his desk going over statements again and nursing a sore head. Shez Mortimer couldn't half knock it back. Vodka, he'd soon learned, was her tipple of choice. They'd spent a good couple of hours in the Wheatsheaf, along with Sam. Not what he'd intended when he left home but a great night nonetheless. He liked her. He vaguely recalled that they'd planned to meet again, although he couldn't for the life of him remember what they'd arranged. Still, he had her card.

"They didn't mention having anything planned. Or did I miss it, Rocco?"

Rocco shook his head.

"The body will be released soon and there's a funeral to organise." Calladine paused tapping a pencil against his teeth. "They're scared. They're running from something or someone."

"Costello?" Imogen suggested. "I'll find out who they've got down there — if anyone."

"If they're running from Costello, what's the link? Why?" He got up and walked to the incident board. "Did you get anywhere with Emily's past?"

"Not really but they did know each other. Beyond that, I can't find anything."

"It's not enough."

The office phone rang. It was Julian.

"Wayne Davey was killed with a single stab wound to the heart. The killer knew his stuff. The blade was long, thin and very sharp. I'd say your killer has had practice."

"Thanks, Julian. Anything on forensics?"

"Yes. Roxy tells me the lipstick used to touch up Emily's make-up isn't available in the UK. Apparently it's French. Also we found a number of hairs on her clothing."

"That's useful. DNA?"

"Possibly. A number of them have the root intact. But it's the length and colour that might be of significance until we get the DNA results back. Long. I'd say chin length. Darker and longer than Emily Blackwell's. Does that help?"

"It could. I'll give it some thought. Thanks again, Julian."

He left the office and knocked on Birch's door.

"Professor Batho has added a little interest to the mix."

"Sit down." She gestured to the chair opposite her.

"Hair was found on Emily's clothing — not hers. I'm presuming it came from whoever laid her out. Expensive,

French lipstick was used to touch up her make-up. Her hair was combed, that sort of thing. And there are prints on her shoes. It will all be very useful when we bring someone in."

"You have someone in mind?"

"Tanya Mallon has chin-length dark hair. She is also the type of woman I can imagine shopping in Paris for her clothes and make-up. But that isn't evidence."

Birch nodded.

"Nonetheless, I want to bring her in and speak to her officially."

"What reason would you give her?"

"All this started the day she arrived. She was on the Hobfield when Davey was shot. We only have her word that she didn't see anything."

"Given her relationship with Costello we should run it past DCI King."

"She'll object," Calladine said at once.

"Let's ask her." Birch lifted the phone and suggested she join them.

"Don't jump down her throat," Birch advised. "See what she has to say. If DCI King does object, then she'd better have a damn good reason."

"Found Archer yet?" asked Eliza King as soon as she entered the office.

She looked drawn, as if she hadn't slept all night. That'd teach her to stay at the Wheatsheaf. He had tried to warn her.

"Forensics on Emily Blackwell's clothing is in," Calladine told her. "Hair and expensive make-up. I'm thinking it could add up to Tanya Mallon. She's one of Costello's PAs or a lady friend — take your pick."

"But you don't know for sure?"

"No. But there is no one else. She was on the Hobfield within minutes of the shooting and she had an interest in Clough Cottage. Plus it's only a matter of time before the forensics are in. If Mrs Mallon is innocent, she shouldn't object to doing a DNA test or giving us her fingerprints."

"What do you want to do?"

"Bring her in. Interview her officially about her whereabouts Tuesday morning. If forensics does get a match she won't be able to charm her way out of that one."

Eliza King ran a hand through her hair wearily. Today it was hanging loose around her face, making her look younger than ever. Calladine couldn't believe they were expecting serious input from a person who looked like some wild teenager.

"I'm not keen on the idea."

"Why not?"

"She's close to Costello."

"Oh, *above-the-law* Costello," he jibed. "We're telling you this out of courtesy, DCI King." He inhaled deeply and waited for the argument to start, but she surprised them.

"Okay. Do what you want."

"Are you okay, DCI King?" Birch asked. "Only you seem a little . . . preoccupied today. Has something happened? Anything we can do to help?"

Calladine fully expected a resounding no, and for Birch to be put firmly in her place. But he was wrong.

"I've had a bad night," she admitted. "That's two on the bounce. That pub I'm staying in is a nightmare. You were right," she said, turning to Calladine.

Calladine hadn't expected that. Lack of sleep had taken the edge off that hot temper. He suddenly felt sorry for her. The woman was struggling. That hard exterior could well be a front. Their work was difficult, as he knew well. She'd obviously worked hard to get where she was. But at what cost, and how much longer could she keep up the pace?

"Do you want to be present at the interview?" Calladine asked.

"No. I've got some problems of my own to sort. For a start I've got to find somewhere else to stay."

"Right then, ma'am. I'll go and find the woman before she disappears."

Eliza King followed him out.

"Have you got anything on Archer and his friends yet?" she asked as they walked back to the incident room.

"Davey is dead and Garrett and Archer have scarpered. But they'll turn up. They need the money they get from dealing on the Hobfield, so it's just a matter of time."

She closed her eyes. "This is doing my head in. I'm shattered. That bloody pub, the case — and problems at home. My mind didn't stop all night."

"Look, if you're really pushed I've got a spare room at my house. It's nothing special. I live in a two up, two down terrace on one of the back streets but despite that, it is quiet."

"If you're serious then yes please. But are you sure? We haven't got off to the best of starts, have we?"

He grinned. "I've got broad shoulders. I'll get you a key from my desk and jot down the address."

* * *

"The well's no good, Annie," Jack Naden told his wife. "It's completely clogged up. The engineer reckons there's been no water in it for years."

"This is serious. We can't do without water, Jack. What does he suggest? What about connecting to mains water?"

"We're too far out and too far up. We've got to get our supply from Clough spring, but how?"

"Couldn't the well be dug out?"

"He says the track of the stream has changed in the forty years since this place was last lived in. It doesn't reach the well anymore. Ideally a borehole is what we need. But that means heavy machinery and a pit for a storage tank digging out."

"Did he give you a timescale?"

"It's not time, Annie, its money we're short of."

"What does your dad say?"

"He's having a word with the engineer. It might be possible to take water from my dad's tank — pipe it down the hill."

"It needs sorting, Jack. We can't get on with anything else until it is."

Then Jacob Naden called out. "Son! The engineer reckons it'll work. We run a pipe straight down that incline there." He pointed to the hill. "The trough can be dug in a day. A small tank sunk somewhere in the back here, filtered then piped to the house."

"Cost?" Annie asked.

"Not as much as the alternatives, lass. My supply is more than adequate. I've told him to go ahead and get the digger up here."

"Will we need planning permission or anything?"

"I'll have a word," Jacob reassured her. "We'll be returning the land back to as it was, so there'll be nothing to see. The tank will be in your backyard."

Annie sighed. "Let's hope nothing else happens to jinx this project."

* * *

"I can't imagine what you think I've done, Inspector." Tanya Mallon sounded faintly amused.

"It's just a chat," Calladine said. "I'd like you to think back to the morning of the auction. What did you do before you went to bid?"

"It was a morning affair, Inspector, and quite early too." She thought for a moment. "I imagine I got ready and had breakfast at the hotel."

Cool as a cucumber.

"Did you visit Clough Hill or the cottage that day?"

"No. I had neither the time nor the inclination."

"Are you aware that we found a body on the hill that morning? Emily Blackwell. Does the name mean anything to you?"

She gasped. "You can't possibly think that woman's death has anything to do with me! I can assure you that's not my style."

"No, but fancy lipstick is."

"Now I'm intrigued. What's my lipstick got to do with this?"

"We have found certain forensic evidence. Currently it is being analysed. Plus we retrieved a good set of fingerprints from Emily's shoes."

Tanya Mallon stood up. Her face was like stone. "I'm here voluntarily?"

Calladine nodded.

"Well, I've heard enough. I'm leaving."

"The evidence we've got could just as easily prove that what you've told us is correct, Mrs Mallon."

"What do you mean?"

"Allow us to take your prints and a DNA swab and you can go on your way."

"No!"

"I can't see why you'd object."

"Well, I do object. You must be desperate if you seriously think I had anything to do with that woman's death."

"Sit down, please. We haven't finished."

She looked around the room. There was a uniformed officer by the door and Rocco was seated beside Calladine.

"Tell me why you won't give us a DNA sample or your prints. Are you afraid of what we'll find?"

Tanya Mallon fell silent. Her face was unreadable.

"Okay. I was there," she said finally. "I was having a last minute look at Clough Cottage and I saw her lying there in a crumpled heap. I went to help her but when I got up close I could see that she was dead."

"Was there anyone else about?"

"No. Not a soul."

"Did you recognise her, Mrs Mallon?"

"No. I'd never seen her before."

"Did you not think to call an ambulance or the police?"

"I couldn't leave her like that. She had mud on her face and grass in her hair. I did it without thinking. I straightened her limbs, folded her arms, did her hair and put some lipstick on her."

"A more normal reaction would have been to call for help. What you did was very strange, to say the least."

"I didn't think. Anyway the dead don't scare me, Inspector. For a short time in my twenties I worked for an undertaker. Fixing hair and that sort of stuff was what I did."

"Even so, it was obvious that she'd been shot. The killer could still have been around. Did you not worry about your own safety?"

"Yes, when I saw a man approaching up the hill. There were trees in the way so he couldn't see me. He was walking along the path towards her, so I left."

"Did you take anything from the scene? We never found Emily's bag or phone."

"No. Come to think about it, I didn't see them either."

"Does this have anything to do with Costello?"

"He's not even in the area. And he has no reason to want her dead. They didn't even know each other."

"Yes, they did."

This didn't appear to faze her and he wondered why.

"I work for Mr Costello *occasionally,* Inspector. I have no idea who his friends are. He could know half the population of this town for all know."

"When do you plan to return home?"

"Saturday." She stuck her nose in the air. "I still have things to do. Can I go now?"

"Not yet. You'll have to give a statement and there is the fact that you interfered with a murder scene. There may be charges. You will have to give us your prints and DNA now — for elimination purposes."

DCI Birch had been watching this from the next room. Once Tanya Mallon had been led away, she joined Calladine. "In my opinion she's hiding something."

"She admitted being there and seeing Emily's body."

"She's still got more to tell. Make sure she doesn't disappear."

Chapter 12

Calladine stared at the incident board. He still had no idea what this was about. He had a dead woman and a dead teenager. Plus a tenuous link to Costello, but nothing that would stand much scrutiny. A motive would help. Emily appeared to have led a blameless life and Davey was small-time.

"We've got another one," Rhona Birch said, sticking her head around the office door. "A body has been found floating in the river under the viaduct. A pathologist from the Duggan is on site and thinks it's suspicious."

"Any idea who?"

"No, but he's young. Calladine, get down there and see what's going on. If we're lucky it'll be a jumper, if not then things are really stacking up.

"What are you thinking, sir?" asked Imogen.

"My gut feeling is Garrett or Archer."

"Rocco is looking at the CCTV from the hospital again. Do you want me to come?"

"Okay. Did you find out if Enid has anyone in Cardiff?"

"Nothing yet, but I'll keep looking when I get back."

Calladine's mobile rang as they were walking out to the car. It was Ruth.

"I've been thinking. I'm stuck here all day and Harry's suddenly decided he likes sleep. I've got loads to do but I'd rather help out with the case." She laughed. "It'll help me remember who I am. If you fill me in, give me some research or whatever, I might come up with something. That fresh pair of eyes we were on about?"

"Me and Imogen are going to the viaduct. There's another body. We'll call in on our way back. Why not give Joyce a ring, get her to email the progress report over. You can have a look and we'll discuss it later."

"I'll put the kettle on."

"You heard all that?" Calladine said to Imogen.

Imogen nodded. "It's a great idea if Ruth's up to it. It would mean me and Rocco could be spending more time on the Hobfield."

Calladine drove along the High Street, past the school to a small roundabout. Here the viaduct loomed above them, spanning both the road and the river. The area had been taped off. A stone wall separated the footpath from a grassy embankment. It was steep, only a slip away from a tumble into the water.

"Take care!" Doctor Bower shouted up. "One of the forensic blokes has already had a ducking."

The Victorian stone viaduct with its high arches loomed above them. Despite the recent warm sunshine there was moss growing all over it. A train thundered across, making the ground vibrate and drowning out the voices of the people working around the body.

Calladine and Imogen inched their way down. It was a young male, lying on his front in the water. The river was low, little more than a trickle. He looked up. The lad could easily have been thrown from the path at the top.

"Knifed," Bower said as Calladine got closer. "His wrists and ankles were tied. There's a lot of broken bones too, legs and arms."

"Chucked down from up there?"

The pathologist nodded. "Probably."

Bower turned the lad over so they could see his face. "There's extensive bruising and a nasty bump on the side of his forehead. His nose has been bleeding."

"Beaten up, knifed and thrown down here for good measure," Calladine said. The young man's face was disfigured from the fall but Calladine recognised it. "We've seen him recently." He called to Imogen who was talking to Roxy Atkins. "It's Mick Garrett."

"One of the three you saw on the Hobfield yesterday — Garrett, Archer and Davey."

"Yes. And today two of them are dead." Calladine stood up and looked around. The viaduct carried the railway line but it ran beside a busy road and above them was a footpath used by walkers. "How long, would you say?"

"I won't know for sure until I get him back but I'd say last night."

"I wonder what he was doing here."

"Meeting someone?" Imogen suggested.

"I want to know if this is where he died or if he was simply dumped," he told Roxy. Then he looked at Imogen. "Killed here means he could have been waiting for someone like you say. Dumped means there had to be a vehicle involved. There's CCTV on the roundabout, it's an accident blackspot. Get Rocco to take a look."

"We'll get him back to the Duggan. You'll have the preliminary by this afternoon," Bower said.

"What are you thinking, sir? The Costello angle again?"

"I can't see why he'd want either Davey or Garrett dead. In all probability they've never even met. Perhaps DCI King can add something."

The forensic team were combing the area. "I'll try and have some answers later!" Roxy called to them.

"If not Costello, who else would want the lads dead?"

"Could be anybody, Imogen, and there's the problem. We've no idea who's making a play for the Hobfield, have we?"

"Costello has to be in the running. Doesn't the car make it obvious?"

"Tanya Mallon offered an explanation of sorts for that one. But I'll see what Doctor Atkins comes up with before I decide. Once the forensics are in on Emily's clothing I'll be speaking to her again." He fell silent as another train thundered over them. "The Hobfield has been quiet of late. A bit of anti-social from the teenagers but nothing to get anxious about. I was beginning to think the place had turned a corner. Seems I was wrong."

"Back to the nick, sir?"

"You go. Take the car. I'll walk back via Ruth's. I could do with clearing my head."

"I'll bring DCI Birch up to speed."

* * *

"I like what you've done with the place." Calladine smiled.

"It's Jake's blackboard from the kitchen. We usually stick all sorts of junk on it. Dental appointments, his timetable, my work rota, but it'll do this job fine," Ruth responded.

She'd set it up as her own incident board in her conservatory. It was all there, a mirror image of what they had back at the nick. But the main difference was that Ruth had put a photo of Vincent Costello slap bang in the centre. She'd also drawn chalk lines between him and all the people involved.

"Tanya Mallon. She's his PA of sorts. The three lads — a big question mark. I don't see where they fit in yet. Unless they were working for Costello and attracted the attention of a rival firm."

Calladine shook his head. "Why? He's retired, getting on. Surely he can do without it."

"You have to consider it, given what's happened to those lads," she said. "Emily Blackwell — she doesn't fit the rival gang theory. She's an old friend from the past. And that's where you need to look, Tom. It's the small details that hold the key. We know they knew each other — Emily and Costello. They used to go around in a group. You need to explore that. Start with Carol, Costello's girlfriend back then. Find her. See what she has to say. And what are you doing about Emily's things? The report makes no mention of any. She'd have had a bag, probably a phone too. Whoever did this may have rung or texted her prior to meeting up."

"You have been busy. I'm impressed. We only spoke about you helping a little over an hour ago."

She smiled and handed him a mug of coffee.

"The truth is, I'm fed up to the back teeth of having nothing to do. I need to work. I look in the mirror and I see this woman I don't recognise. She has a fat belly and a haunted expression. Harry is gorgeous and I love him like nothing else but I can't do motherhood full-time — it'd kill me."

"I for one am pleased to hear it. Your input is missed. I haven't had my mind fully engaged on this. The phone thing — we should have something back from the service provider by now. I'll get Imogen on it when I get back. All we've got on Carol is just that name. There's no surname. Ken Blackwell, Emily's ex, is doing a ten-stretch. He might talk to me about the past, given what's happened."

"Start with him then."

He nodded at the pram. "How's the monster doing?"

"He's discovered sleep. He went off last night no bother. I'm trying to get him into a routine. I can't carry on the way I've been going. I have to take control. This motherhood lark is damn hard. Give me a full-time job any day. How's it going with Monika?"

"We're having lunch Saturday."

"Try not to ruin it this time," she said. "I'm talking about other women, and try and give her a bit of your time."

Ruth's attention was drawn to her laptop on the desk. She'd received an email. "Just a minute." She read for a few seconds then gave Calladine a big grin.

"Costello owns Jet Holdings," she announced proudly.

Now he really was impressed. How had she found that out?

"I've had Imogen routing around for days and she couldn't find anything."

"Companies House, Tom. I have an old friend from college who works there. I asked her to be creative in her search. Jet Holdings is a subsidiary of Rose Argent Enterprises, aka Costello."

Calladine took a closer look at the board. "He was paying Emily money every month — why?"

"You might well ask. He's hardly the type you blackmail, is he?"

"So it must have been payment for something, but what?"

Calladine downed his coffee. "You've been great, Ruth. Wish you could come back full-time."

"It won't be long. I've got a nursery place organised. But I want to help with this. Keep me in the loop and have a word with Birch before she gets on your back about me having all this information at home." She nodded at the board.

"She'll be impressed too, I know."

* * *

Back at the station Calladine brought the team up to speed and set about rearranging their incident board. "Imogen, we need those phone records. The service provider has had long enough. Rocco, anything on the CCTV from the hospital?"

"Nothing useful, sir."

"The phone company said they'll email them through but it's going to be later today," Imogen confirmed.

"Have a look at what CCTV there is from the roundabout near the viaduct. I want to know what cars were in that area last night."

"It'll be some list. That's the main route up to the motorway."

"Can't be helped, Rocco. But given that the pathway is a popular walking spot, start with the footage taken after dark."

Calladine went to find Birch. She was in her office talking to Eliza King. He was about to leave them to it when she beckoned him in.

"The body was that of Mick Garrett, ma'am," he told her. "That leaves Archer out there alone. Now the big question. Is he hiding or is he lying dead somewhere?"

"Plus, who have they upset?" Birch chipped in.

"Emily Blackwell received money each month from Jet Holdings. That company is owned by Costello." He turned to Eliza King. "Do you know any reason why he would do that?"

She looked genuinely surprised. "No. None at all. We thought there might be a connection, given their ages and where they grew up. But we'd no idea about the money. So your research paid off?" she asked.

"Not exactly. The information was down to Ruth Bayliss, my sergeant," he said to Eliza King. "She came up with that little gem and gave me some good ideas about where to go next with the case."

"She's on maternity leave!" Birch exclaimed. "If she's working, it has all sorts of implications."

"It's nothing heavy, ma'am, just a little research from home. Plus she's always been great in the ideas department."

Birch huffed. "We'll discuss that one later. What else has she come up with?"

"That I talk to Ken Blackwell about the past. It was on my list. She reckons I should ask about Emily's friends, particularly one called Carol. We don't know her surname."

"Good idea," Eliza King said.

"He's doing time in Strangeways," said Calladine. "I'll ring them and set it up. Do you want in on this, DCI King?"

She nodded. "Okay."

He looked at her again. "But first we should speak to Costello. We need to know why he was paying her the money."

Birch nodded. "I totally agree."

"I'd prefer we let him be for now," said Eliza King.

"DCI King, he has vital information that might help solve this case," Birch pointed out.

"It will balls up my investigation."

"Not necessarily," Calladine said. "We aren't going to arrest him, we just want information. Given what's happened, he can't see anything untoward in that."

"He'll think we suspect him. That'll put him on his guard."

"Ring this Gavin Trent person and arrange it," Birch decided. "We can't delay. We need answers."

Chapter 13

Calladine and Eliza King pulled up in Strangeways car park.

"Have you been here before?" he asked.

All the way there, she'd sat quietly beside him. She wasn't easy to talk to. All he got back from his attempts were one word responses.

She shook her head. "You?"

He shuddered. "Oh yes. Ray Fallon was an inmate. I had to speak to him on a number of occasions. In fact he died in here."

"I read about that. His wife, wasn't it?"

"The long-suffering Marilyn. Which reminds me, I have a dog, Sam. He'll be curious when you turn up at the house but he won't bite."

"What's your dog got to do with Fallon's wife?" she asked.

"Sam was her dog. She left him with me when she was put away."

"You knew her that well?"

"I was brought up with Fallon."

Eliza King made no comment. Well, let her make what she wants out of that, thought Calladine. He suspected that there were things in her life she'd prefer to keep quiet about. The Costello angle, for one. She knew him, or had had dealings with him before. He'd seen real hate in her eyes when they'd talked in Birch's office.

Having completed the formalities they were shown to a room furnished with a table and four chairs. After a short wait, a prison warder escorted Ken Blackwell into the room. He and the guard sat down opposite the detectives.

Blackwell was tall and thin with dark hair. He looked drawn, as if he never slept.

"I'm sorry about the loss of your ex-wife, Emily," Calladine said kindly. "We are doing everything we can to find the culprit."

Blackwell shrugged. "I haven't seen her in years. She didn't visit, not once. And the boy . . . poisoned his mind, she did."

"Will you go to the funeral? It can be arranged, you know."

"I'm not sure. It's a day out, I suppose. If I can stand the hassle. Her lot will be there. That sister of hers is bound to point the finger and blame me. Like she always did."

"We'd like to ask you some questions about Emily's past, particularly about people she knew. But you are under no obligation."

"I don't mind. I'll try. Though I don't know what I can remember."

"You both knew Vinny Costello."

"Oh, I remember him alright." He looked at Calladine and his eyes narrowed to slits. The memory was evidently uncomfortable. "He didn't kill her," Blackwell said at last. "They had something. I've no idea what, but it got me down."

"What do you mean — something?" Eliza King asked. "Are you saying they were romantically involved?"

He gave a humourless laugh. "Oh no. Vinny only ever had eyes for Carol. She was the love of his life. Emily and Carol were friends. They shared stuff. A lot of it I'd no idea about. But Vinny knew. They were thick as thieves, the three of them."

"I don't think Costello killed Emily either," Calladine said. "Do you know why he paid Emily a sum of money each month? It's been going on for years."

"No idea. First I've heard of it. But it doesn't surprise me."

"Do you recall Carol's full name?"

The warder whispered in Blackwell's ear. Advice? Or was it a warning not to say too much about what went on in Costello's world?

Calladine assured him again. "We're not looking to incriminate you. We simply want to talk to her."

"It's not you lot I'm bothered about," Blackwell grunted.

So he was concerned that Costello might find out about this conversation. That man's tentacles reached everywhere.

"Carol Rhodes was her name. She lived in Leesdon. Don't know where she is now. We all lost touch."

Calladine smiled. "Thanks. That could help immensely."

"The money?" Blackwell asked. "Was it a lot?"

"No, just a small amount. Went up every now and then. Inflation, I expect."

That seemed to satisfy Blackwell but he didn't say why.

The warder coughed. "Ken has had enough now."

* * *

"Carol Rhodes," Calladine told the team. "She was an ex-girlfriend of Costello's. We need to find her and ask what she remembers about Emily's life during those years. Did they keep in touch, that sort of thing? Jet Holdings is

125

owned by Costello. So effectively it was him paying Emily the money every month. We need to know why. Given the number of years it has been going on it has to be something to do with the past."

"Sir!" Rocco interrupted. "CCTV from last night. Guess whose car was parked a few yards from the roundabout?"

Rocco looked pleased with himself.

"Tanya Mallon's," he said. "It was there for a good fifteen minutes. Long enough to do for Mick Garrett."

That woman again! She was everywhere in this investigation. But restrain, beat and then stab Garrett? It didn't fit somehow. "Thanks, Rocco. We'll bring her in. Imogen, see if you can find Carol Rhodes. Marriage records, electoral register, you know the drill." Calladine drew a ring around Tanya Mallon's name on the board.

Eliza King stood watching, hands on hips. "She works for Costello. I had hoped we could soft-peddle things where he was concerned. At least until I've made contact with my informant again."

"We can't wait. Besides it might not even involve Costello. But we can't ignore the fact that she's involved in this right up to her pretty neck. We can't hang around. Give her any more leeway and she'll be gone."

"Costello is bound to find out, and when he does he'll be on his guard. This is going to trash all my hard work." Eliza King stormed back to his office, slamming the door behind her.

"I take it she's not coming with us then. Pity. She'd do well to be a bit more hands on with the case."

"Pennine Inn, sir?"

"Yes, Rocco. It's lunchtime, so with luck she'll be there. If not, we'll have to get uniform to wait until she turns up."

* * *

They were in luck. Tanya Mallon was there, alone. She was talking on her mobile as the two detectives entered the restaurant.

"Hello again, Inspector. Looking for me?" She smiled, putting the phone in her bag. "Work calls me back, I'm afraid. I'll have to cut my visit short."

"We'd like you to come down to the station. Answer a few more questions."

"Can't we do it here, Inspector? I've already ordered lunch and the chef is preparing something special."

Calladine and Rocco sat down. "Where were you last night?"

"In the bar," she replied. "From eight till late, I'm afraid. I got into a conversation with a gentleman from Florida."

"Will he confirm that?"

"He can't. He left for home this morning."

"How convenient. What about the barman? Will he vouch for you?"

"I've no idea where he is today, Inspector."

"Your car was caught on CCTV in Leesdon last night. It was parked at the scene of a murder."

She stared at him wide-eyed. "Another killing? This town isn't safe, is it? I'll be sure not to venture out alone after dark again."

"Can you explain what your car was doing there?"

"No, Inspector, I'm afraid I can't." She thought for a moment. "Something odd though. This morning my car was not where I'd left it. I park in the small car park at the side of the hotel. This morning it was right outside the main entrance."

"What are you saying?"

She smiled. "That someone borrowed it, Inspector. My own fault entirely. I really shouldn't leave the keys in the ignition."

"And you expect me to believe that?"

She shrugged. "It's what happened. Unless you can prove otherwise."

"Did you mention this to anyone?"

"Yes. I told one of the porters this morning. John, I believe his name is."

"There are other factors in this case that I want to question you about."

"I'm sure this is some sort of harassment."

"Not at all. It's just a few questions."

"Are you going to arrest me?"

"No, but your cooperation would be appreciated."

"Then I'm afraid I'll have to disappoint you. After lunch I have packing to do and then I'm returning home."

Calladine was fed up with all this verbal dancing.

"In that case I will arrest you, Mrs Mallon."

* * *

"Anything on Carol Rhodes yet, Imogen?" Calladine had left Tanya Mallon in a soft interview room with two uniformed officers. He needed strong coffee before he tackled the woman again.

"Nothing concrete, guv. She's a mystery. There is an old missing person report from the seventies. Joe in archives dug it out for me. Seems he knew the Rhodes family. We'd be searching forever if he hadn't put it in his special box. Apparently he was never happy with the outcome. Her family decided Carol had run off with her boyfriend — Costello. That might be true but he certainly didn't marry Carol. His wife is Spanish. So why didn't she return home? There were no letters, no phone calls, not even a card at Christmas."

"And her family didn't take it further?"

"No. Joe told me they weren't up to much. But that's not the point. When she disappeared, Carol was only fifteen."

"Where did she live?"

"Back Lane, number three."

"Okay, Imogen. Would you go down there and speak to the neighbours? You never know, one of them might remember her."

"Doctor Atkins rang while you were out. She says Garrett was killed where he was found."

He turned to Rocco. "Ready for this?"

The DC nodded.

Calladine's mobile rang. It was Shez Mortimer.

"Fancy another session later?"

No shrinking violet this one. "What time?" The words were out before he could stop them. He should have refused, made an excuse, so why hadn't he? Because he could feel it starting again. The excitement at meeting someone new and hitting it off immediately. Shez was fun and very attractive. Although she had dark hair, she reminded him of Lydia. He sighed into his phone. This was going to cause no end of trouble with both Monika and Ruth.

"The Wheatsheaf. Get away when you can. I'll wait for you."

Rocco was looking at him sideways. Calladine kept his mouth shut. He didn't want this getting out yet.

"Tanya Mallon was seen at the shooting on the Hobfield and again at the site of Garrett's death. She'd better come up with something better than coincidence this time."

Tanya Mallon didn't seem to be bothered in the least by her detention. As the detectives entered the room she was touching up her make-up.

"A girl has to do her best." She smiled as she put the mirror back in her bag and checked her watch. "Will this take long? I have things to do, Inspector."

"Don't we all," Calladine responded. "Might I suggest you tell us the truth this time and then we can all get on with what we have to do."

"I don't know what you want me to say. I've done nothing. But that doesn't fit with your theories, does it?"

"What were you doing last night?"

"I was in the bar."

"We need the name of someone who can back that up."

"I told you, the man I met has gone."

"The barman then. We can always get the guest's name from the hotel later."

"His name is Robin. You could ring the hotel and ask."

"I'll do that." He nodded at Rocco who left the room.

"Should I have a solicitor present?"

"Do you need one?"

Another charming smile. "No, I don't think I do. Your detective will be back presently and he'll confirm what I've told you."

"You were on the Hobfield the other day and there was a shooting. You were by the viaduct last night and there was a stabbing. Suppose I do believe you had nothing to do with either incident, I still have to ask if you saw anything."

She shook her head. "No. Like I've already told you. This is all quite tedious."

She spent the rest of the time until Rocco returned, staring at a picture on the wall.

"Robin confirms Mrs Mallon's story."

"I told you. I don't lie, Inspector." She gave them both a small smile and began to stand up.

Calladine stopped her. "Not so fast. You can stay here and give the constable a statement."

* * *

Tonight Shez Mortimer wore a fitted navy number with the high-heeled slingbacks. Her hair hung in a glossy curtain and she sported the signature red lipstick. She broke into a wide smile when she spotted him.

"You keep long hours. A policeman's lot, I suppose."

So he had told her. He couldn't remember doing so, but the fact didn't seem to bother her.

"We've got a big case on," he explained.

"I've seen something in the local rag. A woman found dead in a local beauty spot."

"It's turning out to be a tough one and it involves some hard characters."

She patted his knee. "You have my sympathy. My own job can get tricky too. We get our fair share of dodgy punters in the escort business. Particularly those who don't want to pay. Tackle them and they turn into Neanderthals. The wealthier they are, the worse they behave."

"How many escorts do you have?" He had no real idea what was involved or how a business like that would work.

"Currently I'm based in Manchester but I'm looking to expand. I have ten girls on my books permanently and others I can call on if we're busy. It's a lucrative little number, Tom. The hours are okay. I run things from my office day to day but I'm always on my phone if there's a problem at night."

"Do the men always expect . . . well, you know?"

Shez laughed. "Some just want a dinner partner or someone to talk to while they're away from home. As long as they pay the bill, I don't mind."

"But there must be plenty of the other sort?"

"Oh yes. Those who mistake the word 'escort' for something else entirely, if you get my meaning. My girls know the score. They all know what's required and how far to go. Most of them I hand-picked myself. It's picking the punters that takes the skill."

"So you're perfectly reputable?"

She laughed out loud. "Yes, of course. I run an escort business. It's all very tasteful and discreet. How dare you suggest anything else!" She slapped his arm.

"Have you sorted out your employee yet — Annette? The one who was dining at the Pennine Inn?"

"Yes, we've had words. She's seen the error of her ways. It turns out it was a bad night anyway. The customer didn't pay. Robert Silver dumped her in favour of a classy piece with an American accent."

Calladine stared at her. "Do you happen to know the name of this classy piece?"

"No idea. Annette said she cocked her little finger and he went running. Dumped her and left her to pay the bill. A lesson learned, I think."

"This customer of yours. Robert Silver, you said?"

She nodded. Not a name Calladine knew. But he could look it up. "My advice is, keep your distance."

She put her hand on his. "I can look after myself, you know."

Calladine didn't doubt it. "It might be nothing, but the woman he met has been interviewed in relation to a case we're investigating. Just be wary."

"That doesn't surprise me. Robert's no angel. I always got the impression he had a dodgy past and some scary friends."

"Any names?"

Shez shook her head. "It wouldn't do to say. You being police. Some of those scary friends are clients," she explained. "That's how I met him. How far away is your place?"

"Not far."

"Do you have booze at home?"

"Plenty in the fridge and I have a bottle of vodka — unopened since Christmas."

"In that case, want to spend some quality time?" She leaned closer and kissed him on the lips.

Calladine hadn't felt like this in a long time. He got to his feet and took her hand.

Chapter 14

Friday

"He's cute." Eliza King tickled Sam under his chin. "I'll take him for a walk before I go in."

"You don't have to," Calladine replied. "Tea and toast suit you?" He walked off into the kitchen. When he'd come back last night with Shez, he'd forgotten about Eliza King being here. Fortunately she'd been up in her room, flat out he hoped. Shez had left this morning before she'd surfaced.

"Did you sleep okay?"

She nodded. "I certainly did. It's nice here. Far quieter than that pub. I'd have gone mad if I'd stayed there much longer."

"It's always suited me."

"You live alone?"

Calladine called back from the kitchen. "Currently, yes."

"No kids?"

"I've a grown-up daughter, Zoe. She lives with her partner in a new build on the edge of town."

"Hard work, daughters. I've got two. The eldest is nineteen. Gives me no end of trouble, that one."

"You don't look old enough." Calladine placed a mug of tea and plate of toast in front of her.

"It must be down to good genes or something. Because it's nothing to do with lifestyle, believe me. I did everything young. I married, had the kids. I'm not apologising for it, it's how things are. I'm thirty-eight."

"It must have been hard when your girls were little — working, climbing the promotion ladder."

"I managed. But I'm suffering for it now."

Talking about her family had touched a nerve. She went quiet. After a few minutes she grabbed a slice of toast and Sam's lead and left. Calladine had hoped she might start to relax a little. But she was no better. The woman was a complicated mix of the volatile and the moody. Just the type he could do without. Calladine thanked his lucky stars they weren't stuck with her. He checked his mobile. Nothing from Shez. She'd promised to text when she arrived back home, but there was a message from Imogen. Emily's provider had sent over the list. Most of the calls were from friends or Ricky, but several were listed to an unregistered pay-as-you-go. It was the one that had called the ambulance for Wayne Davey.

The bullets were from the same gun, so it should come as no surprise. Emily must have known the caller. Why else would she agree to meet in an out of the way spot?

He tidied up and checked the fridge for food. He made a mental note to buy more milk and left for work. The weather was kind again so he walked. He was trying to pack in as much exercise as he could.

* * *

"Something struck me on the way in," Calladine said to the team when he got to the station. "The Pennine Inn has a CCTV camera at the entrance. It's pointed down the drive. Would you check it, Imogen? See where Tanya Mallon's car was parked up when it returned, and if possible who was driving. Also, would you check if anything is known about one Robert Silver."

Joyce was on the office phone. "Sir, uniform have a young man downstairs. They've just picked him up on the Hobfield. It's Kayne Archer."

"DCI King?" Imogen looked towards his office.

"She's not arrived yet. Last I saw she was walking Sam."

"Will you speak to him?" Joyce asked.

"With pleasure. Let's hope he's got something useful to tell us."

* * *

"How did it go then, you and Tom?"

"We're meeting tomorrow. Before you get too excited it's only the garden centre and a bit of lunch," Monika said to Ruth. "It was being in the churchyard that did it. His parents' grave could do with cheering up. I'm going to help him choose some plants."

"You're good for him, Monika. He might not realise it, but he needs you."

"Yes, but do I need him?" Monika frowned. "He really hurt me, you know. I won't go through that again, not even for him. You tell me he's changed, but he seems like the same old Tom to me. Apart from how he looks, of course."

"I think he's learned his lesson. No excuse I know, but he's a sucker for a pretty face. He knew Lydia wasn't for keeps. She was using him to get a story. In the end it cost her her life and Tom feels guilty."

"Well, I'll give it a go. But I'm keeping it friendly. I'm not prepared to hop into bed like the old times. Not until he proves he's a reformed character."

"That's fair enough."

"What does he want — Reverend Philips?"

135

"He's got a couple of questions."

"You go in and I'll walk Harry around until you're finished."

"He should be okay, he's asleep." Ruth clapped her hands gleefully. "Things are looking up."

Monika had pushed baby Ireson around the graveyard several times before Ruth resurfaced.

"The reverend is long-winded. Harry been okay?"

"Not a peep."

"Someone you knew?"

They were standing by Agnes Jackson's grave. Fresh flowers had been left that morning.

"I'm puzzled, that's all. She had no one, so who's leaving these?"

"Soon find out." Ruth ducked down and read the card that had been left. "*My one true love*," she read. "There you are then — an old boyfriend."

"Not Agnes. She lost her husband when she was in her fifties and was glad to be rid. She wouldn't get involved again."

Ruth took a closer look at the inscription on the headstone. "There are two of them in there. Agnes Jackson, who died a year ago and her mother, Doris, who died in 1969. Perhaps the flowers are meant for her."

"I doubt it. How old would the old codger have to be? Agnes's mother was sixty when she died."

"It's bugging you, isn't it?"

"It's weird, that's all. If Agnes was still alive I could have asked her. I don't know who would know now."

"It could be a simple mix-up. A case of the wrong grave." Ruth noted down the names and the dates. "I'll ask the vicar later. He might be able to tell me something."

* * *

Kayne Archer was shown to an interview room to wait. He was edgy. He kept looking round as if expecting to meet someone he didn't want to see.

"She in yet?" Rocco asked Calladine as they watched him through the two way window.

"No — and she'd better not have done one with my dog either."

"You think Archer is her informant?"

Calladine nodded.

"How does that work then? What can he possibly know about Costello?"

"I'm not sure that he knows anything, Rocco. All I do know is that he and his mates have upset someone. Costello? A rival firm making a play for the Hobfield? Who knows? He had a gun on him too. It's gone to the Duggan. Julian should be able to tell us if it was the one that killed Emily and shot Wayne Davey."

"She won't like it if we muscle in."

"In that case, Rocco, she should get in on time. Come on then. Let's get this started."

"Mr Archer," Calladine began with a smile. "Careless of you, getting picked up like that. Didn't you realise you were a marked man?"

Kayne Archer was tall and thick-set. His complexion was swarthy and pock-marked and he looked older than his nineteen years. He wore the regulation denims and hoodie of most of the crew off the estate. The hood was pulled over his head. He looked as though he didn't want to be seen. Who could he be afraid of here in the nick?

"Davey and Garrett are dead," he grunted.

"How do you know about Garrett?"

"Word's out. Some rival gang got them both."

Calladine smiled. "Rival to who? Costello? You must have got that wrong. Whoever killed your mates doesn't have a beef with Costello. He rarely operates around here these days.

"I'll be next. I need protection."

Short and sweet. And avoiding an answer.

"Why? Who are you afraid of?"

"The whole bloody lot of them." There was real fear in his eyes. "Costello, because he thinks I'm a grass. The firm who want to take over, because I'm in the way."

"Costello has no interest in you."

"He'll come after me. He thinks I know things. He wants to shut me up."

"Who have you been working for, Kayne?"

"I don't know. This rival gang — whoever!"

Calladine knew that Archer wouldn't feel comfortable talking to the police like this. He'd try his best to get away with saying very little. He was only here at all because it was safer than being on the street.

"I can't help you if you don't talk to me."

Archer appeared to wrestle with this for a few moments.

"We could bail you — send you back out there and see what happens," added Calladine.

"Costello wants the estate."

"Why? Who told you that?"

"A bloke said he could use the three of us. We stood to make a lot of money."

"Who is this man?"

"He works for Costello."

"Are you sure about that?"

Archer nodded. "He knew things, about jobs Costello and him had worked on."

"Tell me about the gun, Kayne. Start with where you got it from."

"He gave it to me."

"The bloke who works for Costello? Does he have a name?" Calladine asked. "And think carefully because it could make all the difference to where you spend the next few decades of your life."

Archer's head shot up. He looked Calladine in the eye. "I didn't use it. I never shot anybody. No bullets, you see. We were going to do a trade for the weed, but things never got that far."

"Not much use, is it, a gun without bullets. Who was this bloke who gave it to you?"

"I dunno."

Calladine tried another tack. "You said Costello thinks you know things. What things, Kayne?"

The lad looked Calladine in the eye. "That's just it — I don't. It's all one big scam. I was paid to contact the police. I was told to talk to a DI King. I was to make out that I knew stuff, something that'd stitch Costello up good and proper."

That much Calladine could believe; it was why Eliza King was here. But who would gain from this charade?

"Who told you to do this, Kayne?"

"Never gave me no name. Said it didn't matter."

"The same bloke who gave you the gun?"

"No. It was a woman."

"You'd been recruited by Costello's people. Why double-cross him? You must have realised that was a dangerous game to play."

"I thought I could handle it. She offered me a lot of money too."

"Did you get paid?"

Archer shook his head. "Only a bit. I was supposed to get the remainder once it was done."

"When did you know it was a scam?" Calladine asked.

"When I couldn't contact her anymore."

"Do you even know if there is such information?"

Another shake of the head.

"Who is she, Kayne?"

The lad stared at his hands, which he'd placed flat on the desk top. "I don't know her. I've never even seen her. She always texted me."

"Back to the bloke who recruited you and your mates. He gave you a gun. Handed it to you, I presume. So come on — what did he look like?"

Archer was back staring at his hands. He didn't want to talk. But he wasn't stupid. Calladine was counting on him realising that if he had any hope of walking away from this, he had no choice but to give the police what they wanted.

"He didn't give me the gun. He left it for me. He put it in a carrier bag and left it on the common. In a bin."

"When was this?"

"Same day Wayne got his kneecaps done."

"So come on then, what did he look like?"

"Like I said, I didn't see much of him. He was tall, thin and wore a suit."

Calladine was getting frustrated. "That description could fit half the blokes in this town. I need more, Kayne. Is there anything that's different about him?"

"He has half a finger missing." Archer rubbed the little finger on his right hand.

"How does he contact you?"

"By mobile. He gave me one to use but I got rid of it. I don't want anything to do with this anymore."

"That was a stupid thing to do. The phone could have helped us find this man."

"Never mind the phone. I need locking up for my own protection. I've got Costello's goons after me for ducking out. Once they find out that I was working for that scary cow too, I'll be a goner."

Calladine could barely restrain his laughter — a scally off the Hobfield asking to be locked up!

"Can you tell me anything else about the woman?"

"Nowt except she's careful."

"Okay, Kayne. This is what we'll do. A colleague of mine will want to talk to you. The DI King you mentioned. So we will keep you here. Get the lad a cup of tea," Calladine told the uniformed officer.

Calladine and Rocco returned to the incident room. "You don't think he shot Emily, sir?"

"No, Rocco. Archer is merely a pawn in this. It would appear that both sides are using him. But I still can't get my head round the idea that Costello would want the Hobfield."

"Archer seems pretty sure, sir."

"He's in a lot of trouble. If the gun was the one used to shoot Emily, and we don't come up with an alternative, things are looking bleak for him."

A quick glance through the glass partition into his office told him that Eliza King still hadn't turned up. He went to the board and drew a large question mark in the centre. Then he spent the next few minutes bringing Imogen up to speed.

"I reckon this mystery man with the missing finger has been orchestrating events," he said. "But unless Archer can come up with something useful to help us find him, we're stumped. And then there is the woman. What does she hope to gain, I wonder?"

Imogen nodded at his office. "He might speak to DCI King. They must have built some sort of relationship. In the meantime, I'm off to speak to neighbours of the Rhodes family, if I can find some." She grabbed her bag.

"Hi, folks — been missing me?" It was Ruth. And she was carrying Harry. "I've had to leave his pram downstairs — no lift." She passed him to Joyce who was holding her arms out.

"I'm here to see where you've got to with the case," she explained.

"I don't think Birch is keen on you working while you're still signed off," said Calladine.

"Fair enough but if I just happen to glimpse something, well, I'm bound to comment, aren't I?"

"In that case you can *glimpse* this." He handed her the statement Tanya Mallon had made. "She interfered with Emily's body. No explanation that holds water and she insists she didn't take her phone or bag."

Ruth read and then waved it at him. "This is a load of rubbish," she said. "You're in a strange environment and you find a dead body. A body with a bullet hole in the

141

chest, I should add. Not to mention with blood all over it. What would the normal reaction be?"

"I made the same point. Tanya Mallon said she didn't think. That she just wanted to wipe the mud from her face. She used to work for a firm of undertakers so it was no big deal."

"Rubbish! Most folk wouldn't go near. They'd check whether the person was injured but once they realised they were dead, and particularly when they saw all that blood, they'd shy away. They'd most definitely call for help. They certainly wouldn't wipe faces, touch up make-up and fiddle with hair. The woman's lying, Tom — has to be. She knew Emily. Not only that, Emily Blackwell was someone Tanya had sympathy for."

"There's nothing in their backgrounds to suggest that."

"I've told you, you're not going back far enough."

Chapter 15

"I'm DC Goode from Leesworth CID," Imogen introduced herself to Mrs Hunter. "I'm looking for people along here who remember the Rhodes family."

The elderly woman frowned. "What is it with that lot? Has one of them come into money or suddenly become famous?"

Imogen smiled. "Not that I'm aware of. It's just part of an investigation we're carrying out at the moment. I'm particularly interested in—"

"Carol Rhodes. You don't have to tell me. You and half this town it seems."

"Has someone else asked about her?"

"That young woman, Annie Naden, was knocking on doors earlier in the week. She's the one that bought Clough Cottage. She came round here twice asking questions. I can only tell you what I told her. I've no idea where Carol went. You lot investigated back then so you must know more than me. Her bloke was that thug, Vinny Costello. Her parents decided she'd run off with him and dropped it."

"Why was the woman from Clough Cottage interested?"

"She said she'd found something belonging to Carol. If you want to know more, you'll have to go and ask her."

"Are there any of the Rhodes family left?"

"Parents are dead and I've no idea what happened to the boy — Carol's brother."

"Do you recall his name?"

"Darren. He was a year or two older than Carol. Bad lot. He was into drugs even back then."

"Is there anyone else along here who would have known the family?"

"No, love. I'm all that's left from them days."

"Thanks, Mrs Hunter. You've been a great help."

Imogen had already knocked on every door on the street. Most folk were out. But from what she'd just been told they wouldn't be able to add anything anyway. She had no choice. Like it or not she'd have to visit Clough Cottage again.

* * *

"Sorry about the noise!" Jack Naden bellowed at Imogen. "We're having work done for the water supply."

"They're digging a trench right down the hill?" Imogen was surprised.

"Clough Stream doesn't reach the well anymore," he explained. "So we're having water piped from my father's source."

"Not on the mains?"

He laughed. "Not up here, love. The well used to do the job. It was piped in, stored, then fed into the cottage. My dad gets the farm supply from a borehole that feeds a huge storage tank. We'll be okay once the work's done."

Imogen was relieved that she and Julian had lost the bid. Goodness knows what this little lot was costing. And if they had placed the winning bid, Jack's father might not have been so accommodating with them.

"I'm from Leesworth CID," she told him, showing her badge. "It's your wife I want to speak to."

"She's in th' house. What's it about?"

"A satchel she found."

"Bloody thing. She's gone on about little else since she found it. Help yourself — mind the rough ground."

It was odd being back here with all the work going on. Imogen had come to view the cottage with Julian on a warm spring evening. It had been peaceful then. It was in a lovely spot and she'd been smitten. But they'd had a lucky escape. Perhaps there was something to be said for a semi down in Leesdon. At least it would have running water on tap.

"Annie Naden?"

The young woman turned around. She was about Imogen's age and had short blonde hair. Her clothes were covered in a mix of paint and plaster.

"Look at the state of me," she said, trying to rub the dirt from her shirt.

Imogen flashed her badge. "It's about the satchel you found."

"I've been meaning to bring it in. At first I thought I might find her — Carol, the girl it belonged to. But no one knows where she is."

Annie went to a large pine table where the satchel lay. "Here. Everything is in there. A selection of schoolbooks but, most interesting, her diary. From what she wrote Carol Rhodes seemed like a nice enough girl. I found it in a cupboard behind the panelling over there. Someone must have hidden it all those years ago."

"Thanks, Annie. We're hoping this might help with a case we're working on. And if we're lucky, we might find her or a relative we can give it back to."

"If you do, let me know. I read her diary. It's funny but I almost feel as if I know her. She was a typical teenager — head full of boys and going out." She smiled. "I do hope she's okay."

"Why do you say that?"

"No one has seen her in years. She simply upped and left. That's not usual for someone with a settled home life, is it?"

"My bloke and I bid on the cottage, you know," said Imogen, changing the subject. "You, me and that woman nobody knew."

"Sorry if you had your heart set. But in a way you were lucky. When we bid, we had no idea about the problems, or the history." She shuddered.

"The problems I can see well enough, but I know nothing about the history of the place."

"A woman lived here, forty odd years ago. She wasn't popular. Granny Slater, they called her. She carried out abortions in this very kitchen." Annie folded her arms, shaking her head in disgust. "Possibly even right here." She slapped her hand on the old pine table. "It's given me nightmares, I can tell you, since I learned that. We've got no choice but to live here now. But if I'd known before the auction I wouldn't have bothered."

"I'm sure it'll be fine. You'll make it your own. You are talking a long time ago. A lot of the old houses around here will have history."

"What with that and the palaver with the water it's really hard. All that going on out there had better work. I can't even wash. There's nothing comes out of the taps. That was something I hadn't thought of."

"Our forensic people will want to take a look at the place," Imogen said.

"The place is in such a mess it hardly seems worth it."

"You'd be surprised what they can find. It'll be the cupboard the satchel was in that will interest them the most. I'll let you know if we find Carol." Imogen made to leave.

"You don't think she came here for a . . . you know — an abortion?" Annie asked her. "Like I said, I read her diary. Carol was pregnant. It was the last entry she made. There was nothing after that."

Imogen suddenly felt cold. Perhaps Annie was right and the place did have ghosts. An abortion? It was certainly possible.

* * *

Tanya Mallon was in the bar when Calladine and Rocco arrived.

"You caught me, Inspector," she said, raising a glass of red wine. "What can I do for you now?"

"You can tell me the truth." He nodded towards a table. "Shall we sit down?"

"I've told you everything I know."

She followed Calladine and Rocco to a table.

"I'd like you to go over what happened when you saw Emily lying on the hillside for me once again."

"You can be a real bore at times, Inspector. I don't know what else I can tell you."

"You recognised her. The pair of you had history."

She laughed out loud. "What an imagination! How could I possibly have known her?"

"I don't know yet, but you did." Calladine sounded certain but he had nothing to back this up other than his and Ruth's gut feeling. "Your reaction to seeing a dead body was all wrong. When you saw who it was things changed and you got stuck in."

"A bit of lipstick!"

"I don't buy it. The woman had been murdered, shot. Her clothing was bloody, and she'd been beaten. You happen along and set about fixing her face . . . Come on."

"I didn't see it like that."

"Where do you come from, Mrs Mallon?"

"I live in New York, have done for years. Hence the accent," she smiled. "My husband's job was there, so we moved."

"Where is he now?"

"Greg is dead and buried, I'm afraid."

"Where did you live prior to New York?"

147

She sipped her wine. "I've lived all over the world. I've been lucky. I married a man who was well able to provide for me, and provide he did."

"But you were born around here." Another stab in the dark.

Her eyes narrowed.

"I think you knew very well who Emily Blackwell was and you felt sorry for her."

Her face was like thunder. "Prove it."

"Come on, Mrs Mallon. Where were you born?"

She shook her head. "Completely irrelevant."

"We can easily find out. Won't take more than an hour or so."

She glowered at them both. "You do that. I refuse to be interrogated like this."

"Who is Robert Silver?" Calladine could see Rocco looking curious. The DC would be wondering why he'd suddenly pulled that name out of the hat.

Tanya Mallon looked from one detective to the other. "I have no idea."

"You and he ate here the other night."

"I've met a lot of people since I've been here. Other guests, the manager and a number of the barmen. We talk, we have a glass of wine and sometimes we eat together. I don't remember them all."

"Back to Emily Blackwell. She was a friend of Costello's. He knew her from years ago when they both lived in the area. So where do you fit in, Mrs Mallon?"

"It's very simple — I don't. As I told you."

And Calladine couldn't prove otherwise — yet.

* * *

"Dom, I want you to check something out."

Eliza King was sitting in the kitchen of Calladine's house talking on the phone to Sergeant Dominic Shevlin. "That number we had for Gavin Trent — it's gone dead. I'll text it to you. Would you find out who the service

148

provider is? I have a horrible feeling that we've been fed a shedload of lies."

"Surely not, ma'am."

"The case is falling apart. The informant has disappeared before he had the chance to tell me anything useful. I'm being pushed to set up an interview with Costello and I can't contact Trent."

"Costello?"

"Yes. His name has come up in a case the team at Leesdon are working on. DI Calladine doesn't suspect Costello of anything, but he thinks he could clear up one or two details."

"Can't you contact whoever put you onto Trent in the first place?"

"No. He contacted me and that's the problem. It was a couple of months ago when we were working on that big drug case in Hull. Costello's name was being bandied about, and next thing I get a phone call from Trent. I should have handled things differently but it was a way in and I grabbed it. The problem is that if I can't raise Trent then the team here will approach Costello directly. And if they do that they could really balls things up. If our informant does have anything to give us, then I want it."

"Do you think Trent knows what you're up to? Could that be why he's pulled the plug?"

"I don't see how he can. We are a tight team."

"No chance the informant will turn up?"

"I can't call it. If he's got any sense he'll have scarpered. I know I would. Someone is on to him. Two of his mates have been killed."

"In that case Costello knows," Dominic Shevlin said. "He'll not rest until he's secured his position again. Did you get anything at all from the informant?"

"No. The last time he called we were going to meet when I got to Leesdon. All I know is that whatever he wants to tell us can put Costello away for the rest of his life. We need that information, Dom. We have all worked too long and hard on this to simply give up now. But that said, I don't know how to proceed . . . Did you call in on the girls?"

"Yes. Becca's fine but Jade wasn't there. Becca says she's going to her auntie's until you're back."

"Jade is with him — Harvey Evans. I'm worried, Dom. She won't listen to reason and I'm sure she's using again. If this case goes pear-shaped that's something Costello can use. Evans works for him, don't forget."

* * *

"DCI King? A word, please," Rhona Birch called out as Eliza King passed her office door. "We have Kayne Archer in custody. DI Calladine spoke to him earlier." She handed over the statement.

Eliza King read through the document and slammed it down on the desk. "He maintains it was all a put-up job? I don't understand. We had an arrangement. We've talked numerous times. He's lying, trying to wriggle out of it. This is cold feet, that's all."

"Calladine thinks he's telling the truth."

"Calladine doesn't know the Costello case or the informant like I do."

"Nonetheless, before you dive in there I want you to talk to Calladine. In fact the pair of you can interview Archer together next time."

Eliza King was reading through the statement again. "If Archer has been spinning us lies, then all the work my team has put in has been for nothing. We were promised information that would lock Costello away for good." She was furious. Her face was red, her voice full of venom.

"We all agree that Costello is a villain who should have been put away years ago. You'll get no arguments from anyone here on that one. What I don't understand is why this affects you so much." Rhona Birch waited for Eliza King to say something. "When we first spoke,

Calladine said this was personal. I think he's right. Is there anything you want to tell me, DCI King?"

Eliza King shook her head. "You're wrong. I'm just doing my job."

"Don't speak to that young man alone," Birch warned as she left the office. King was lying. There was more to this than she was telling. "There is to be a briefing in fifteen minutes. Make sure you're there."

Chapter 16

DI Calladine, Rocco, Imogen and DCI Birch were seated around a table in the large meeting room. Joyce was taking notes.

"DCI King should be here," grumbled Birch. "I don't like her lone-ranger tactics and I'll tell her so when she turns up. She hasn't been near Archer, has she?"

Calladine shook his head. He passed round copies of a short report on their progress so far.

"I've spoken to Superintendent McCabe. He thinks it's a good idea if someone speaks to Costello. I think that someone should be you, DI Calladine. DCI King is too personally involved in my opinion. Though don't ask me how because she's not saying."

Calladine's stomach jolted. Interview Vinny Costello. He wondered how that would pan out. His nerves began to jangle.

"You okay, Inspector?"

"Yes, ma'am, why wouldn't I be?" He winked at Imogen. "Apologies for the report being a little sparse. We have to gather a lot more background information. We need to know about Tanya Mallon's past for a start. She has a connection to Emily and to Costello. I don't buy what she told us about finding Emily's body. My gut feeling is that she's from around here and knew Emily. So who is she? We should also ask if she's the woman Archer told us about."

"I'll look into her past, sir," Imogen offered. She checked the notes Rocco had made when they'd interviewed her. "Her husband's name was Greg. I should find her maiden name from the marriage records."

"She may not have married in this country. She's lived for a while in the US."

"No worries." Imogen was scribbling on a pad.

"We now have an old school satchel belonging to Carol Rhodes. It's gone to forensics. I've asked them to look at the diary first and pass on anything that will help the case."

"Annie Naden read it, sir. The final entry was on the sixth of May, 1969. Carol wrote that she was pregnant."

"We know Clough Cottage was where girls went for an abortion. You've been told that, Imogen, and I was too by someone who lived in the town at that time. Is that what Carol did? Is that why her satchel was there?"

"There is no one left to ask, sir," Rocco pointed out. "The woman who lived there — Mary, or Granny Slater as she was known, is long gone. Even if she's still alive we'd have to find her."

Rocco was right. But there was someone who might have the answer to this — Costello. He'd been Carol's boyfriend. What was the betting that he was also the father of her unborn child?

"Forensics?" He looked at Imogen.

"The Nadens are not happy, but that kitchen is being taken apart as we speak. The satchel was found in a cupboard built into the wall panelling. Finding it at all was a piece of luck."

At that moment Eliza King entered the room. She nodded at Birch and sat down.

"You can start compiling a list of things I need to speak to Costello about," Calladine told the team. He looked at DCI King. "Nothing heavy. We simply want information about Carol Rhodes and what happened to her."

Eliza King cleared her throat. "Gavin Trent has let me down. I can no longer reach him on the mobile number he gave me."

"We don't need him. McCabe will sort things for us," Birch told her.

"When did Trent first contact you?" asked Calladine.

"A couple of months ago."

"And Archer?"

Eliza King's eyes went wide. She grimaced. "Yes. About the same time," she muttered.

"It could have been Trent who recruited Archer for Costello. Did you ever meet him?"

"No. We only ever talked on the phone."

"Is this important?" Birch asked.

"Could be, ma'am. He could be the mystery man who's missing half a finger."

"We will liaise directly with Costello's legal team. And DI Calladine will do the talking," Birch said in no uncertain terms.

"I'm not sure we should speak to him at all, Tom." Eliza King spoke directly to Calladine.

Rocco nudged Imogen. She'd just called him *Tom*. Was she coming round?

"Why are you so concerned about what happened to this Carol?" Eliza King asked him. "Surely something that happened forty-odd years ago can have little bearing on Emily Blackwell's murder."

"It's a line of enquiry Ruth Bayliss suggested. Personally, I think she's right. I don't know what, but something happened in the past that has a direct bearing on recent events."

"There is nothing in Emily's life that offers a clue. She was spotless," Imogen added.

"Well, there's the money from Jet Holdings," Birch reminded them. "The payments started in June 1969. We have no idea what the money is for and neither does her family. But Jet Holdings is Costello. When DI Calladine speaks to him perhaps he'll clear that one up too."

"I'll be sure to ask him," he said. "I'll be surprised if he's very forthcoming. But something happened in that cottage back then. My gut instinct tells me that whatever it was led directly to Emily's murder a few days ago."

Birch nodded. "Very well, Calladine. We'll run with this for now. But don't forget we also have two dead young men. Again, no motive and no suspects. If we don't clear that one up soon we'll have the super on our tails."

Rocco was checking his phone. "Tanya Mallon's car was driven last night, sir. The CCTV caught it returning to the hotel, just as you thought. The quality of the footage isn't good. All we got was a shadow of a figure."

Calladine explained to Birch. "She spun us a tale about her car being taken and returned."

"When will you speak to Costello?" Eliza King asked.

"As soon as he agrees," said Birch. "He is merely being asked to provide us with information. He is not under suspicion, so I see no reason for him to refuse."

* * *

"It's done through Joe, the odd-job man. He picks up the flowers from the shop and brings them to the grave. You should talk to him. He's been here far longer than me. Before him, it was his father who did all the jobs around the churchyard."

"So the flowers thing was sort of passed down?" Ruth asked.

"That's right."

"But no one knows who they are from. Don't you find that odd, Reverend?"

"I can't say I've ever really thought about it. Families do all sorts of things. There is a grave in that far corner that has tomato plants growing on it for most of the summer."

"I'll find him and see what he knows," Ruth decided.

Ruth pushed Harry around until she spotted Joe. He was tending a flowerbed full of glorious blooms. "You have green fingers," Ruth said.

"And you have your hands full," he answered, peering into the pram. "Having him christened here?"

Ruth nodded.

"You local?"

"Yes. I've got family going back to the nineteenth century in here somewhere," she replied. "Plus two on the war memorial."

He smiled. Her answer seemed to please him.

"Agnes Jackson. Do you know who leaves the flowers?"

"I do."

"Did you know her — Agnes?"

"No, but the flowers aren't for her. They're for Doris, her mother. I collect them from the florist every week. But I expect that'll stop now she's dead."

"What do you mean?"

"Mrs Blackwell paid for the flowers. That woman that got shot up on the hill. I just chose them, picked them up and put them on the grave."

"Did you ever speak to Mrs Blackwell? Ask her about the grave?"

He shook his head. "I knew her of course but it was her business, not mine."

"And this has gone on for some time?"

"All the way back to when her mother died."

"What about the card, Joe? Who decided what should be written on it?"

"Mrs Blackwell did. The florist wrote it. It was always the same words."

"Weren't you ever curious, Joe? Did you ever talk about this to anyone else?"

"It was none of my business, Miss. Mrs Blackwell paid me and I did as she asked."

Ruth took another look at the grave. "How do you know the flowers were for Doris?"

"Who else could they be for? There's only the two of them in there."

"When was this dug?"

"The date's on the headstone. May 1969 for Doris. My father will have dug it."

"Once they've been prepared are the graves ever left open and unattended?"

"We put a barrier up overnight." He smiled. "Stop people falling in."

"Thanks, Joe. You've been a great help."

This mystery went back years. Whoever started the flowers thing didn't want their identity known, so they'd got Emily to organise it. She rang the nick and Imogen answered. "The graveyard in Leesdon Church," Ruth told her. "Flowers are left regularly on the grave of a woman, one Doris Ludford. This has gone on since 1969. She's buried with her daughter, Agnes Jackson, who died about a year ago. The interesting bit is that during all this time the flowers have been paid for by Emily Blackwell. She didn't do it herself though, she paid the odd-job man here to pick them up for her. Would you check if there's any connection between Doris Ludford and Emily?"

"1969, you say? What date exactly did Doris die?"

Ruth checked her notes. "May Seventh."

* * *

The first thing Imogen did was to check with the florist in Leesdon. Emily Blackwell had paid for the flowers by direct debit each month.

She handed Calladine the information from Ruth. "You should see this. I don't know what it means. I've

157

checked if Emily knew this Doris or had any connection with the family, but I can't find anything."

Calladine looked at the date. "The entry in Carol Rhodes's diary?"

"The last entry was the day before, sir. It was one word — 'pregnant.'"

"Great work, both of you. Anything on Tanya's past yet?"

"I'm still searching. How old would you say she was?"

"Fifty or so. But she's well preserved. She's done some maintenance — not like me." He rubbed at his stubble. "I'm nipping home in a bit for a proper shave. It was a bit of a rush this morning and I've got DCI King staying."

Imogen shot him a speculative look.

"No, you don't," he warned. "The rumour mill is bad enough around here. Before you get any smart ideas, she was staying at the Wheatsheaf before. What was I supposed to do?"

"Sir!" Joyce interrupted, holding out the office phone. "Professor Batho."

"Tom, the gun has been used before. Way back in the late sixties it was used in a robbery at a post office in Oldston. No one was killed but a customer was winged in the leg. The bullet was retrieved from the wall and has been kept in storage ever since. The striation marks were on the database."

"Why, if no one was killed? It wasn't a murder investigation."

"The investigating team at that time believed the gun belonged to Vincent Costello. He was in on the robbery. A witness statement has him wielding the thing but the details are sketchy. Other evidence that would have convicted Costello was botched or disappeared, including the gun. So he walked. They hoped to gather further evidence if the gun was used again. But it never was. Not until recently."

"When in the late sixties?"

"November '68."

"So it wasn't definite that Costello owned the gun or that he'd used it?"

"No, Tom. The team made mistakes. Once the case got to court the defence made mincemeat of them. However, there is one interesting fact. The gun was reputed to have Costello's name written on the barrel."

"Now why would he do that?"

"Bravado, showing off. Possibly it was the first gun he owned. There could be a hundred and one reasons. Costello was young and foolish back then."

So where had the gun been all these years? This case just got more complicated as information came in. "Thanks, Julian. I'm sure it'll be useful somewhere down the line."

Something else to ask Costello about? Calladine wasn't sure. It would change the interview from being an affable information-seeking exercise into something else entirely. A gun from Costello's past? If they could prove that, and prove he'd used it, then they would have him. But how likely was that?

Calladine spent the next few minutes updating the incident board. He still couldn't make sense of it. An event in the past involving Carol Rhodes had led to the death of Emily Blackwell a few days ago. Somehow Tanya was involved, but he'd no idea how. And why did the two lads from the Hobfield have to die? On top of all this was Kayne Archer and the information he was supposed to have. His head ached.

"I'll be back in half an hour. I'm on my mobile if anyone wants me," he told Imogen and Rocco, and left.

* * *

The walk home took him down Leesdon High Street. Calladine spotted Ruth coming out of the chemist. She was on her own.

159

"Where is he?"

"With Jake — inset day. Harry came to the church with me but now I need to do some serious shopping."

Calladine didn't like the way she was looking at him. Her tone was even, but there was something on her mind.

"Great work you did," he said. "I don't know what it means but I don't doubt we'll find out."

"It seems straightforward enough to me. Emily Blackwell set up the flower thing with the money from Jet Holdings," she told him. "So ask Costello why."

"That is just supposition. The money went from Jet into Emily's bank account. She had a separate direct debit for the flowers, so we can't prove it."

"I've been talking to Shannon, the barmaid at the Wheatsheaf."

This could be trouble. Ruth wasn't happy and it didn't take much brain-power to work out why. This was scarier than his impending interview with Costello. "Gossip, eh?"

"Yes, and not the type I wanted to hear. You were in there last night."

It was no use denying it. "So?"

"You were with a woman, a woman Shannon didn't recognise. The pair of you were very friendly. At one point you even kissed her."

"Actually, *she* kissed me." He shuffled uncomfortably, his hands in his pockets. "I'm a big lad now. I am allowed to see women, you know."

She leaned towards him. "Monika!" she hissed. "Or have you forgotten about her? If she gets the merest whiff of this it'll really piss her off, and you'll have blown it for good. You may not appreciate it, Tom Calladine, but this is your last chance with her. She won't stand for any more of your messing around."

"I couldn't help it."

"You never can."

There was an awkward silence. Calladine felt like a prat.

"So who is she?" Ruth finally asked.

"Just a woman I met when I was out walking Sam. She's good fun. I like her."

"Is she local?"

"No — Droylsden, Manchester."

"So what brought her to Leesdon?"

"Work."

"What does she do?"

"She runs an escort agency." He crossed his fingers. Would he get away with that one?

"What sort of escort agency?"

Nope, he wouldn't.

"You know. Escorts . . . dinner dates for lonely businessmen . . . she says it's all very tasteful."

"Hmm, sounds like a euphemism for the sex trade, then. And Monika? What are you going to do about her?"

"No, it's not! It's a perfectly respectable business that she runs. Shez is nice. You'd like her. Me and Monika . . . we're just being friendly. I like her, I always have but she's . . ." He shrugged. "Just . . . Monika," he added lamely.

"You've let me down. Do you realise how hard I worked to get Monika onside? The christening plans are one thing, but I spent a lot of time talking about you. I convinced her that you would be up for giving it another go. I thought you were up for it too, when I saw how well you were getting on. You are good together."

He grimaced. "I'm no good for any woman, Ruth. Never was, never will be."

Chapter 17

"So why feed me all that crap?" DCI Eliza King waited for Archer to reply. "Why all the rubbish about having something on Costello that would put him away?"

Archer looked from one detective to the other. He did not reply.

"DCI King has a point," Calladine added. "You're not stupid. You know the reputation Costello has. Despite that, you agree to front this operation. Presumably you accept money from the woman. You must have known that if he got wind of what you were doing, Costello would come after you."

"Suppose," he whispered.

"It must have been a lot of money you were promised, lad. That, or she had something on you."

Archer shook his head vigorously. "It was nowt like that!"

"This woman. Who is she?"

Archer looked at Eliza King and shook his head. "I don't know."

"More crap! Of course you know. You're not that stupid."

"We never spoke. It was all just texts. She reckoned the police would move in before Costello had time to do anything. There was a couple of things to put in place, people to talk to, then it would start."

"Who did she want to talk to?" asked Calladine.

"I don't know."

"You're going to have to do better than this, Archer," said King. "We are investigating three murders. Two of the victims were close to you. You were arrested with the gun that killed Emily and shot Davey in your possession. If you're not careful you'll find yourself in the frame."

"I had nothing to do with shooting anybody!" He spat out the words. "Wayne and Mick were my friends." His eyes flitted around the room. "I think it was the Blackwell woman she went to see," he admitted at last. "You know, Ricky's mum. She had something the woman wanted. I don't know what — just that it was important."

"Back to her name. What did you call her?"

Archer shook his head. "Didn't call her anything."

"Think harder," King insisted.

"I've told you everything I know," he said.

"Did she ever mention anyone else?" asked King.

He did not reply.

"Shouldn't have been so quick to get rid of the phone, should you?"

"In one text she warned me not to get involved with someone, a bloke."

"What bloke?"

"She called him *Trent*."

* * *

"Gavin Trent." Calladine wrote the name prominently on the incident board and underlined it. "He's been in Leesdon recently. He was DCI King's contact and he's the bloke Archer reckons he was warned about by our mystery woman." He stood back and looked at the jumble of words that filled the space in front of him. "What we need to know is, why?"

"Doesn't he work for Costello?" asked Rocco.

"We don't know for sure. He could be the bloke who recruited Archer and his mates. Always providing we are running with the idea that Costello wants the Hobfield of course."

"And if he doesn't?"

"Then I'm stumped. Kayne Archer is approached by two people. One, a woman, wants to set him against Costello. And promises to furnish him with information he can take to the police. The other, possibly Trent, wants to recruit him and his gang for Costello. The woman? Ideas anyone?"

"Tanya Mallon," Imogen said at once.

"They know each other certainly. They could be bosom buddies for all we know. This recruiting thing, though. I still don't see it. Costello doesn't want the Hobfield. He's way past running drugs on run-down estates."

"Could it be personal?" Rocco suggested.

This had them all thinking.

"The woman has a beef with Costello?" DCI King postulated.

"Possibly," said Calladine. "Or perhaps this is all some elaborate takeover bid. Get rid of the big bad boss and rule the empire in his place."

"Are we going with Trent meeting Emily on that hill?"

Calladine wasn't sure. "Archer thinks his mystery woman met Emily. But he could be spinning us a tale."

"Why would he?" asked Eliza King.

"Because, DCI King, we piled on the pressure in there."

She folded her arms and turned away.

"But then again it might make sense. Emily knew Costello. They had maintained some sort of relationship all these years. She could have known things — secrets from the past."

"We could do with finding Ricky and Enid," Rocco said.

Calladine nodded. "Imogen — any luck with Cardiff?"

"No. They got off the coach at the bus station and then disappeared. I've got the local police checking with taxi firms, but it's a long shot. I did have better luck with Tanya Mallon though."

Calladine went to look at her computer screen. "Tanya Mallon married Greg Mallon twenty years ago," he read. "Her maiden name was Slater. She was born Tanya Slater in Leesdon. No father on the certificate but her mother was Mary — our abortionist."

"She's from around here. So she knows people. She could have known Emily," Eliza King said.

"There is a difference in their ages," Imogen reminded them. "Tanya was only six years old in 1969. Emily would have been in her teens."

Calladine shook his head. "So what does it mean? Why didn't she just tell us? It's probably the reason she bid on the cottage."

"Perhaps, but was it sentiment or to cover someone's tracks? Tanya may have known that there was stuff still hidden there. Carol's satchel, for example. Costello could have sent her here to get it back," said Eliza King.

She had a point. "We need to bring her in. Rocco — send a couple of uniforms up to that hotel to fetch her."

"Alternatively, your theory that she's working with Trent to bring Costello down could be correct," Eliza King continued.

"Why do you think that?"

"I don't know, Tom, but it's a possibility."

"Arrange for a plain clothes officer to hang around up there for a while. Let's see if this man Trent makes an appearance," he told Rocco.

He turned to Eliza King. "Is there anything else you can tell us about Gavin Trent? Any little detail that will help us to identify him? We already know he has half a finger missing. We know he's tall and thin, but that's about it."

She shook her head.

"I would recognise his voice," Imogen told them. "I spoke to him, remember."

"That could be useful," Eliza King noted. "Tom, what do we do about Archer?"

"We hold him."

"Do we charge him?"

"Not yet. He didn't kill Emily nor did he knife the others, but he is mixed up in this."

"Okay — another twenty-four hours." She stood and walked away into his office.

"Sir!" Imogen said. "That name you gave me to look up. He's clean but his son was quite a character."

"Was?"

"Yes, sir, he was killed on a robbery. That Cheshire robbery actually."

Calladine looked at Imogen's computer screen. Robert Silver's son Ryan had a police record. "He was quite a bad boy, wasn't he?"

Imogen pointed to a paragraph. "And he was a known associate of Vinny Costello's. How do you know about him?"

"A piece of luck," he replied. "Print it out for me. I'll look at it closer. He took the sheet and sat at Ruth's desk. Prior to the Cheshire job, Ryan Silver had been in prison a couple of times for robbery with violence. There was also a note about the Costello connection.

"Calladine!" It was Birch. "Costello is coming in this afternoon, at about two. You and DC Rockliffe can speak to him. Do not involve DCI King," she said firmly. "I get the distinct impression that would cause real problems."

This afternoon! He needed some strong coffee.

"You feeling alright, guv?" asked Imogen. "Only you've gone green."

"Do you blame me? This has to be handled exactly right. We get this wrong, make Costello think he's under suspicion and he'll make sure no one can talk. People will disappear. You all thought Fallon was evil. Well, Costello is far worse."

His headache was back. He ducked out into the corridor and rang Ruth. "Are you busy this afternoon?"

"No. Want some help?"

"I want you to hang around the graveyard for a bit, from about two this afternoon. We've got Costello coming in. I want to know what he does when he leaves here."

"You think he'll go there? Why?"

"Just a hunch. Let's see if I'm right . . . Rocco, we'll get a drink and discuss tactics." On the way down to the canteen Calladine's mobile rang. It was Shez.

"I've got the night off," she said in a sultry voice. "I'm all yours if you want me."

Normally Calladine would have piled on the charm. But Rocco was at his side.

"What's wrong? My favourite detective not up for a heavy night out?"

"It's not that. It's the case. We're really stretched."

"You don't work all night. Come on, Tom, we'll eat and then round the night off back at yours."

"Not shy, are you?"

"You've a lot to learn about me, Tom Calladine. I don't hang about. I see, I like, and I go for it." She paused. "You don't mind, do you? Or am I wasting my time?"

"No, not at all. It'll be good to see you again."

"Okay. I'll text you later. If you don't mind, I'd like to know a bit more about Robert Silver. We can eat at that new Italian."

Rocco was grinning. "That didn't sound like Monika, sir."

"I can just about get away with saying it's work," said Calladine. "That woman knows Robert Silver. I want her to talk to me."

"Who is he?"

"For the time being Silver is simply a person of interest."

"And your lady friend?"

"A woman I met the other night when I was out walking Sam. We ended up going for a drink in the Wheatsheaf. Problem is, Ruth found out and now she's on my back about Monika."

"Is she involved in any of this?"

"No. And I'm not even sure that Robert Silver is. But he is staying at the Pennine Inn and he knows Tanya Mallon."

They sat at a table in the corner of the canteen with two strong coffees and a notebook.

"We have nothing on Costello," Calladine reminded Rocco. "He is coming here voluntarily so we must keep it light. We need to get him to talk about Emily and Carol. He might know where Carol is and he might have an idea why Emily was targeted like that. We know he had a soft spot for Carol, so I'm hoping he'll talk to us."

"He doesn't usually help the police, sir."

"I know, and that's got me thinking too. Birch will have given his legal people an inkling of what this is about. Something has touched a nerve — Carol Rhodes I suspect."

"Can we do this, sir?"

"Yep, Rocco. Piece of cake."

Calladine just wished he felt as confident as he sounded.

Chapter 18

It was decided to use a soft interview room, one which had sofas in it. Calladine and Rocco sat on one, leaving the other free for Costello and whoever he brought with him. A pot of fresh coffee and cups had been placed on the table between the two.

Rocco smoothed his dark hair back from his face. "I wish they'd get here. My nerves are strung tight," he said.

"How d'you think I feel?"

"Have you ever met him?"

"Once, years ago when I was a DC. He was brought in for questioning. I recall feeling sorry for the poor DI who had to deal with him. Costello bawled at him for hours. In the end the team got nothing and he was released. What I do remember though, was the way Costello looked at that DI as he left." He shuddered. "I was convinced he was a marked man."

Voices could be heard along the corridor. The door opened and a uniformed PC showed two men into the room. Calladine and Rocco got to their feet.

"Good of you to come." Calladine smiled and held out his hand, which both men ignored.

"I'm Malcolm Hall, Mr Costello's legal advisor. You're lucky. Mr Costello has business in the area so this is not inconvenient. I hope you've no objection, but the remainder of the team are at the end of the corridor."

Remainder of the team! Calladine took a peek as he closed the door. Two of the largest goons he'd seen in a long time were guarding the corridor door.

Costello said nothing. He stood with his back to the wall, his hands in his trouser pockets, chewing gum. Rocco looked scared.

"Sit down. I'll get us some coffee," Calladine offered.

Costello didn't move. Malcolm Hall took a seat, unzipped a leather folder and took out a mobile. "Coffee isn't required. This won't take long. If you have no objection I will record the interview." He placed his mobile on the arm of the chair.

"Fine with me," Calladine replied.

"You're kin of Fallon's," Costello said at last.

Calladine saw a nerve twitch in Rocco's cheek at the sound of that voice. The young detective was terrified. He saw no point in a long explanation of the Fallon thing, so he nodded.

Costello chuckled. "Karked it in Strangeways. You lot must be gutted — no trial, no glory at finally getting the big man."

Calladine said nothing. Costello sat down.

He was a heavy man with broad shoulders. Although he was in his late sixties he had a full head of dark hair. His face was deeply lined and tanned and his eyes were small and piercing. Those vivid blue eyes would miss nothing. He was wearing a dark suit with a silk scarf around his neck instead of a tie. It was warm in the room. Costello unwound the scarf and tossed it on the table where it lay like a puddle of spilt cream.

Calladine had met the man before so he knew what to expect. He saw his DC's eyes widen with surprise. Costello had a very realistic tattoo of a serpent slithering up his neck. It was wide and done in the blackest ink. It appeared to crawl out from under the collar of his shirt and its body coiled around his carotid artery. But it was the snake's head that had caused Rocco to start. It seemed to rest against his jawline, mouth open about to strike, with teeth dripping venom and forked tongue extended.

"What's this about?"

Costello's voice was gruff, deep — and he had a broad Manchester accent.

"I believe you were a friend of Emily Blackwell, or Emily Mason as you would have known her then."

"Yeah, I knew Em. We knocked around together back in the day."

"You also knew Carol Rhodes?"

"Did I?" A cold smile. "What is this, a walk down memory lane?"

"Emily has been murdered and we can't find Carol."

"I heard about Em. I'm very sorry. I'll do what I can to help. Look out for the boy. But Carol?"

"Do you know what happened to her?"

"No. You're talking years ago."

"You were close, I think."

Those strange eyes met Calladine's. "She was the love of my life. I loved the bones of that girl, always have."

Calladine was taken aback at this. "So what happened?"

"Her parents," he said simply. "They didn't approve of me. They poisoned her mind. Suddenly she was gone and I never found out where."

"Couldn't Emily help?"

"She'd no idea either. Carol disappeared and cut all ties with Leesdon."

"She was pregnant at the time. Did you ever wonder what happened to her child?"

Costello's eyes moved from one detective to the other. "Who told you that crap? Carol was never pregnant.

She only ever went out with me. We were kids. We never even . . . you know . . ."

Calladine sighed. All rubbish. Nothing but a string of lies. What Costello said sounded plausible, but none of it was true.

"You have been paying Emily an amount of money each month for years. Why?"

The advisor leaned towards Costello and whispered something.

"It's okay, Malcolm," he said. "You really have done your homework, Inspector. You must have rummaged around in my business accounts to come up with that one. I'd watch my step if I were you."

Calladine could have told him that Jet Holdings was a limited company and therefore its accounts were in the public domain. But he didn't.

"I gave Em that money because she was strapped," said Costello. "She had the kid to raise and a waster of a husband. She was a mate — well, she had been in the past. It was no big deal. I'm a generous man."

Who was he trying to kid?

Rocco was scribbling away in his notebook.

"Do you know what Emily used that money for?"

Costello shrugged. "Rent. To put food on the table. I didn't tell her what to do with it."

"It may surprise you to know that she spent a good part of it on flowers." Calladine paused, waiting for a reaction. But there wasn't one. Costello's face remained impassive. "What do you think about that?"

"Fair enough. She was free to use it for anything she wanted."

"Did you and Carol ever go up to Clough Cottage?"

Costello's eyes narrowed. He flexed his fingers. Calladine sensed that for two pins he'd deck him. He'd known very well what went on up there.

"Now, why would we do that? What are you getting at, Inspector?"

"Nothing in particular. But given Carol's condition . . ."

Without warning Costello banged his large fist on the coffee table, sending the cups jumping to the floor. His eyes held Calladine's. "Carol was not pregnant! Have I made myself clear?"

Calladine returned his look. "Odd that. We got the information about the pregnancy from Carol herself."

There was a pause. Those evil eyes were now mere pinpricks. The advisor had folded his arms, waiting. "I will not tell you again. She did not have an abortion. She was never pregnant. Neither of us ever went near that batty old woman."

Calladine smiled. "I see."

"I hope you do, Inspector. For your sake."

Was that a threat? It certainly felt like one. "It was a long time ago. You may have forgotten. Difficult sometimes to recall every little detail." Calladine couldn't help himself. He was winding the man up, seeing how far he could push him. But Costello had had enough.

"Time to go," he told Hall. "There's nothing more I can tell you."

"Can? Or won't." Calladine jibed.

Costello was just about holding it together. The man's short fuse was well documented.

"Don't get clever with me, Inspector. You've had your interview. Now leave it."

Hall checked his mobile, whispered something to Costello and showed him the screen

Calladine went to open the door. "Thank you for coming in. Did you like the photos Tanya took?"

Costello was putting on his scarf. He stopped and looked at the detective. "Who?"

"Tanya Mallon. You hired her to take some photos of Leesdon for you. She's done a great job. Her stuff is good."

"I've never heard of the woman. Whoever she is and whatever she's told you — it's all lies."

* * *

Rocco collapsed back onto the sofa. "That is one scary man. And that bloody snake! I wouldn't want him on my tail, I can tell you. And what's with you, sir, goading him like that?"

"I couldn't stop myself," Calladine told him. "And it was only a fraction of what I wanted to ask him."

"The questions." Rocco waved his notepad. "You didn't ask about the grave."

"Don't worry. If he has anything to do with that grave, we'll know shortly."

Birch stuck her head around the door. "How did it go?"

"He told us nothing. The money he paid to Emily was to help out, and he hasn't seen Carol since they were teenagers. And he insists she wasn't pregnant."

"Do you believe him?"

"Not for one second."

"I was listening in," she told him. "You were pushy. I wonder how wise you were to take him on."

"He was hiding something. Costello didn't want to talk about Carol or the money he gave Emily."

"The Tanya Mallon bit was interesting. If she isn't working for Costello, what is she doing in Leesdon?"

"I think he was telling the truth on that one, ma'am. I'll get some answers when she's brought in."

"Those men he brought with him. Evil-looking pair. Is that how it always is with him?"

"Costello never ventures out without protection. Even at his age and retired. He has too many enemies."

"This is a police station, Calladine. Surely he feels safe here?"

"Obviously not, ma'am. You saw his bodyguards."

* * *

174

Ruth pushed Harry in his pram down the High Street and onto the park. She sat on a bench overlooking the church. From here she could see anyone who entered the graveyard. Calladine had said sometime after two. She checked her watch. Hopefully it wouldn't be much later. Harry would need feeding again soon.

The grave was significant. They hadn't discussed it but Ruth knew that Calladine was thinking along the same lines as she was. It was the date it had been dug that had confirmed it.

A limo stopped at the roadside. Ruth felt the butterflies start. This was it. Calladine's hunch had paid off. She started to walk towards the church. There were plenty of people around. Plus she couldn't look less like police if she tried. So why the nerves?

There was a whole bunch of them. A tall thin man held back while the man she took to be Costello, surrounded by a group of men in suits, strode towards the grave of Doris Ludford. Ruth stopped a few yards away and tucked Harry in. She watched as Costello knelt and placed a bouquet of red roses on the grave.

She had her phone ready. The tall thin man was speaking on his own phone with his back to her. Costello's attention was on the grave. He appeared to be talking quietly to himself. His minders were hanging back, their eyes on the street. This was her chance. Ruth took the photo.

She walked past the villain without giving him a second look, and back out onto the High Street. She paused for a few minutes by a bus stop and texted the photo of Costello to Calladine. Job done.

Chapter 19

"I want to open the grave of Doris Ludford and Agnes Jackson, ma'am."

Rhona Birch looked up from the paperwork on her desk. "I hope you have a damn good reason, Calladine. First you drag Costello in here and now you want to open graves."

"The minute he left us Costello went to the churchyard and put flowers on the grave in question." He showed her the photo Ruth had taken. It clearly showed Costello, as well as the inscription on the headstone.

"You had him followed?"

"No. I had Ruth on standby. A casual walk through town . . . a stop-off at the church."

"You must have suspected?"

"Yes, ma'am. Doris Ludford was buried the day after I reckon Carol Rhodes disappeared. The grave would have been dug and ready. Ruth has spoken to the man who knows about such things. It would have been open overnight until the service the next day."

"What do you think happened?"

"Carol's abortion goes wrong. She dies at Clough Cottage and Costello buries her in that grave. He'd only have to dig a little more, put her in, then cover her. The following day in goes Doris and the grave is closed."

"It's a big ask, Calladine."

"I think we should take the risk, ma'am. Why else would flowers have been left each week for all these years? He told me himself that he loved her. That's why Costello went to the grave today. He couldn't resist the opportunity."

"And you're sure he's not related to either of those women?"

"Quite sure, ma'am."

She sighed. "There'll be paperwork. And there will be the bishop to deal with. It's consecrated ground. I'll speak to the legal team and to McCabe, see if we can rush this. Leave it with me."

* * *

Imogen shuddered. "That's a new one for us."

"If Carol Rhodes is down there and she'd died at Clough Cottage, what happened to Mary Slater?"

"That is a good question, Rocco," Calladine said. "We'll ask Tanya when she's brought in."

Calladine's phone rang. It was the desk sergeant to say that Tanya Mallon had arrived.

"Imogen, do you want in on the Tanya interview?"

Rocco had taken off his suit jacket and was downing his second coffee since the Costello interview. He'd need a while to get his head together.

"Yes, sir. I'll get my notes."

"She's a cool one," Calladine told her as they strode down the corridor. "This time she should be more willing to talk to us. Tanya will be aware of the significance of us knowing her true identity."

"Nothing back yet on her prints or DNA?"

"There's nothing on the system."

"Do you think she had anything to do with the murders, sir?"

"I don't think she carried them out personally, but she knows who did. We are looking for Gavin Trent and she knows him too."

"How do you know that?"

"DCI King asked for a meet with Trent about the limo on the Hobfield. The next thing we know, Tanya is ringing Birch asking to speak to me. Trent had to have told her. She then spins me the yarn about the photos."

"But we still don't know what this is all about."

"I'm hoping that after our chat with Tanya we'll be in with a chance, Imogen."

"Where've they put her?"

"The downstairs interview room."

"Tom!" It was Eliza King. "You've spoken to Costello! Why wasn't I told?"

"You didn't miss much, believe me," he replied. "He was scary, guarded and we got nothing."

"That's not the point. This is my case." She was angry again.

"We only asked about Carol Rhodes. Your investigations have not been compromised."

"My investigations were compromised the day you lot blundered in," she said angrily.

"There never was any evidence against Costello. Archer has admitted as much. It was a put-up job. Although I can't work out why anyone would bother. Do you want to speak to Tanya Mallon?"

Eliza King nodded. "I'm not missing this one."

Ah well, thought Calladine. She has every right.

* * *

Tanya Mallon looked as if all the stuffing had been knocked out of her. Calladine was trying to work out what was different about her and then he realised — no make-up.

"Do you want a solicitor, Mrs Mallon? We can get one for you."

She shook her head. "Waste of time, the lot of them."

Calladine made a note.

"They virtually dragged me out of the shower," she complained. "Treated me like a common criminal. My hair is still wet."

"We know who you are," Calladine said straight off.

"I could have told you but I didn't see the relevance."

"It's highly relevant. We are investigating a murder, Mrs Mallon. A murder which is connected to events that happened in the past. Your past."

She inhaled deeply and looked at the three faces staring back at her. She smiled at Eliza King. "I like your hair. I've always thought red hair was so attractive."

"Now that really is irrelevant," said the DCI.

"You told us lies," said Calladine. "You do not work for Costello. Back to the day Wayne Davey was shot. You were on the Hobfield and it had nothing to do with Costello. What were you doing there?"

"I showed you the photos. Don't they speak for themselves?"

Calladine was fast becoming irritated. "The photos are not important. That isn't why you were there."

She smiled. "I say it is."

"Do you remember living at Clough Cottage?" Imogen asked.

Tanya regarded Imogen for a moment.

"I remember some of it. But you have to understand I was very young. Some of my memories of that time have become mixed up over the years."

"Your mother. Were you aware of what she did?"

"Yes," she said. "Even at that young age I knew it was wrong. She disgusted me, the things she did to those girls."

"You saw?"

"Sometimes," she admitted. "I used to hide. My mother never knew."

"That must have been hard. Confusing for a small child."

Tanya nodded. "When there were no girls she was fine. She'd play with me. She wasn't very good at motherhood though. There wasn't much discipline. Most of the time I ran wild. But I did love her. When she disappeared, I cried for days."

Calladine sat back and let Imogen get on with it. She seemed to have a rapport with the woman. She'd got her talking which was more than he could do.

"Did you know Carol Rhodes?" Imogen asked.

Tanya Mallon's face was expressionless, her eyes glazed. She was somewhere else. "I think it was her that last night. The night everything changed."

"Will you tell us what happened, Tanya?" Imogen asked gently.

"Do they have to stay?"

"Yes," Imogen told her. "But speak to me. Imagine that there is only the two of us in here."

A few seconds passed before Tanya spoke. "There were three of them, two girls and a boy. I didn't like him, he swore a lot. My mother was seeing to one of the girls. The Carol you're so interested in."

"What makes you think that?"

"She was wearing a school uniform and had a satchel on her back. She left it on the sideboard. When things went quiet I hid it."

"Where did you put it, Tanya?"

"In a special place, a hidey hole in the panelling. I looked inside. Her name was on the books."

"Do you know who the others were?"

"Emily. She was kind to me that night. I was upset and she took me home with her, to a flat on the Hobfield. She gave me food and let me stay. She lived with her sister. She was kind too."

So Enid Mason did know more than she'd said. Why hadn't she told them? Who was she afraid of — Costello?

180

"And the boy?"

"Vinny Costello. He had the gun."

Calladine interrupted. "A gun? Did he use it?"

Tanya flashed him a look. "Yes. At first he was waving it around a lot. But then my mother got shot." She closed her eyes. "She wasn't up to much but she didn't deserve to die like that. What happened to Carol — it couldn't be helped."

"Did Vinny shoot your mother?"

"I don't know. I can't remember clearly. I think there was a struggle. Emily was angry with him. Carol was on the kitchen table and she didn't say anything or move."

"Tell me about the struggle," said Calladine.

"I can barely remember."

"Take your time. Just give it a try."

"I was six years old, Inspector. I was terrified. It was dark. There was a lot of shouting. It was a dreadful experience. It's haunted me all my life. I want it to end, but it won't until my mother's body is found."

"Anything else?"

"Costello was angry, I remember that. He kept swearing at my mother. He wanted her to fix Carol. He kept pointing that gun at her. Emily tried to take it from him but it went off. I saw my mother drop to the floor and then I ran and hid."

"You're doing very well," Imogen said. "Do you know what they did with Carol?"

"A van came to the cottage. Vinny put her in and they left."

"Did you see who was driving?"

She shook her head.

"Your mother? Did they take her away too?"

"No. She simply disappeared. I've never seen her from that day to this. When it went quiet I crept back into the kitchen. Emily was cleaning up. That was when I took the satchel and the gun."

"You took the gun? What did you do with it?" Calladine asked.

"I was going to put it with the satchel in the hiding place but Emily took the gun off me."

"Do you know what she did with it?"

"No. She said it was dangerous. I presumed she gave it back to Vinny."

Tanya was crying. Imogen handed her a tissue from a box on the windowsill. "Would you like a break?"

Tanya nodded.

"Okay, I'll get you some tea."

Chapter 20

They were back in the incident room.

"Do you believe her?" Eliza King asked.

"Yes," Imogen replied. "It ties in with what we know and suspect.

"The bit about the gun?"

"Emily could have taken it. In fact she could have hung on to it all these years," Calladine told them. "I'll lay odds it's the same gun that was used to kill Emily and shoot Davey. Julian has matched the marks on the bullets to a gun used back in the sixties and allegedly owned by Costello. Has the one found on Archer been sent to the Duggan?"

Imogen nodded.

"What do we do with Archer if it turns out it is the same gun?"

"The fact that Archer had a gun at all puts him in the frame. The problem we've got is that it's been used in a game of pass the parcel for the last few days."

Imogen nodded. "If Emily had the gun, she must have given it to someone. Did that someone shoot her with it?"

"We could spend all day speculating on this." Calladine went to the incident board and wrote down the names, one below the other. Trent, Mallon, Archer and finally, Costello. "Want to add anyone else?" he asked the team. "We don't know who had the gun before Emily and Davey were shot. We know someone gave it to Archer. He told us it was after the shootings. The question is — how did Archer's man get hold of it? A man Archer says recruited him to work for Costello. We'll give Tanya a little longer and then we'll ask her about Gavin Trent."

"What about him?" asked Eliza King.

"How she knows him and what they've been up to for a start."

"You think they've been working together?"

"Yes. Trent is our mystery man. The man who's lost half a finger. We need to find him."

* * *

Costello was sitting in the bar of the Pennine Inn.

"How long ago since this Trent guy was last seen?"

"Within the last hour, Mr Costello," the barman told him. "He has been here all week. Spent a lot of time with an American woman. They went out together, ate together. They were close."

"Do you know her name?"

"Tanya Mallon."

Costello's eyes narrowed. He'd heard that name before. That was the woman the detective had asked about.

Costello's driver joined him. "The manager is organising the rooms, sir."

"You did make it clear that I don't know how long we'll be here?"

"Yes, sir. He's fine about it."

"Go see to the baggage."

"It doesn't look too bad a place," Malcolm Hall said. "Good range of food on the menu, adequate bar and the rooms are a fair size."

"See what you can find out about the Mallon woman. Nice it might be, but I don't want to spend an hour longer here than I need to. Give me a whisky," he barked at the barman. "What do I call you?"

"Robin, sir."

No matter where he went, Costello always drew attention. He was a big man and walked with a swagger. He looked exactly like what he was — a villain. The temperature in a room went cold as soon as he entered.

He'd only been at the bar a few minutes but silence had already descended. There were half a dozen people seated around the room. All of them eyed him with suspicion.

He slapped down a twenty. "Keep the change, Robin."

"I believe Mrs Mallon has been arrested, sir," the barman told him. "A couple of hours ago. A detective from the local station has been on her tail all week."

Costello tossed the liquid down his throat. "Does Trent know?"

"I shouldn't think so. It's at least three hours since I last saw him. He was headed towards the golf course."

"Thanks." He slammed the glass down on the bar. "Stick a big one in there." He peeled off another twenty from a roll. "The hotel's course, is it?"

The barman nodded.

"Go find him," Costello told Malcolm Hall. "Tell him I want a word. I'll be sat over there. And sort out a brief for the Mallon woman. You know the drill." Costello took his drink and went to sit down.

He needed to sort this thing with Trent but he wasn't in the mood. Talking about Carol had touched a nerve. Even after all this time the memory was still raw. He thought he'd dealt with it, sorted all the emotional stuff years ago. But obviously he hadn't or he wouldn't be feeling so bad now. Emily had done a good job. The flowers, keeping quiet, getting on with her life as normal. So what had gone wrong? He couldn't work out who would know enough about what happened that night to put Emily in the frame. But someone did.

It had been Emily, Ken Blackwell — who'd driven the van, and himself. There was no one else. Emily was dead but what about Ken? Costello was sure he knew nothing. Ken had no idea who had been put in the back of that van and he'd never asked. But had he found out? Costello took his mobile from the inside pocket of his jacket and tapped in a number. "Job for you," he said. "Ken Blackwell, Strangeways." He ended the call.

He leaned back in the chair and ran through the events of that night in his mind. It hurt to remember. His head was full of Carol's screams and that woman's lack of interest. He'd taken her back into that kitchen and laid her on that table. The woman hadn't touched her. It was already too late. He'd tried to force her to help. He'd threatened her with the gun. Emily had tried to stop him. Next thing the woman dropped like a stone. They never did work out who'd actually pulled the trigger.

Suddenly his blue eyes lit up — the kid! There had been a kid in the kitchen that night, a girl. The woman had sent her away but she could have witnessed it all. Was she Tanya Mallon?

"He isn't there. The golf pro here says he hasn't seen him. In fact he's never even heard of him." Hall sat down beside Costello. "Just had a phone call. Trent's been a busy boy. He recruited three of them. Two are dead — knifed, but the third is in custody."

"That bloody copper again!"

"Trent recruited them in your name. You are apparently taking over the Hobfield now that Fallon's dead."

Costello bellowed with laughter. "No one in their right mind would believe that."

"Perhaps — but it has caused ripples. A prominent Manchester villain dived in without waiting to find out if the rumour was true or not. The prospect of having you back made him very unhappy indeed."

"Stupid fool. All he had to do was ask me."

"Well, he didn't, did he? What he did instead was take a pop at one of our people as a warning."

"Some bloody nerve!"

"Nerve or not, Vinny, Carl Grogan is dead. Shot on his own front doorstep a week ago."

"This needs sorting. Quash the gossip before this gets out of hand. See to it. Meet with people, set them straight. I do not want a turf war on my hands."

"Leave it with me, Vinny. What about the other problem?"

"That isn't so simple. I've no idea what Tanya Mallon knows. She'll have to be dealt with."

"She may have already spoken to that detective."

"So what? There won't be a case if she can't go to court."

* * *

"Tell us about Gavin Trent," Calladine began.

"I don't know anyone with that name," Tanya Mallon replied.

"You're lying."

"I've had enough." She brushed back the hair from her face. "You drag me in here and expect answers, when I have none."

"Trent could be our killer."

Her eyes met Calladine's.

"He had a gun. We have it now and it's being processed," he said.

Now she looked frightened.

"He was staying at the hotel," she said finally. "We had dinner one night. He was pleasant. There was nothing in it."

"I don't think you met by chance. You both came here for a reason. Want to tell us about it?"

"No. There's nothing to tell. He was just a visitor, on his own like me. We ate dinner together a couple of times."

Calladine left the room abruptly. Out in the corridor he rang the Duggan and spoke to Roxy Atkins. Tanya had been quick to talk once he'd mentioned the gun. He thought he knew why.

"The gun we sent over. Would you check it for prints first? See if any of them match Tanya Mallon's. I'd appreciate this doing quickly. We're interviewing her now. A text will do if you get a match."

Calladine went back into the room.

"I want to leave," said Tanya.

"Tell me all you know about Trent and we'll think about it."

She became quiet. Calladine watched her. Something had her worried. Was it the gun? Was that the reason she'd been reluctant to give her prints? Had she handled the thing?

"We spoke to Trent ourselves a couple of times. He was DCI King's contact for all things Costello. I last contacted him when I wanted to speak to Costello about your car. It's registered to his company. And suddenly you are on the phone wanting to talk to me about the photos you took." He watched her eyes widen in fear. "Trent told you to ring us, didn't he? Between the pair of you, you concocted the tale about being on a mission for Costello. But Costello has never heard of you."

She sniffed. "I had to say something. You didn't seem interested in the truth. Coincidence, that's all it was. I read about the shooting in the paper. I'd been on that estate. I knew you'd be looking for my car and I guessed you'd jump to conclusions." She shrugged. "I am not lying to you, Inspector."

"So why the tale about Costello? Why bring him up at all?"

Silence.

"Because that car you were driving around in belongs to Costello. You knew we'd find that out quickly."

"I thought it was Trent's car."

"Is Trent one of Costello's people?"

"I've no idea."

"I have a young man in custody who says he is. In fact he told us that Trent is in Leesdon to recruit new people for Costello."

"I know nothing about that."

"You have an old grudge to settle with Costello. You blame him for your mother's death. But what is Trent's beef? Want to tell me? Because I think the two of you got together and decided to get even."

"Rubbish!"

His mobile bleeped. The text from Doctor Atkins confirmed what he suspected. There was a partial finger mark on the gun — Tanya Mallon's.

"We might yet charge you with murder, Mrs Mallon."

"I've done nothing."

"Your prints are on the gun that probably killed Emily Blackwell."

She started to cry. Imogen shot Calladine a look. She obviously thought he was being too hard on Tanya.

"I don't think Gavin Trent is his real name," Tanya said, dabbing at her eyes. "But I didn't care who he was. All these years I've suffered because of that night. The memory never leaves me. I see my mother fall dead to the floor and I hear that girl's screams. I'd wanted to get even with Costello for years and Trent offered me the opportunity. He contacted me about a month ago. He said he had a proposition that I couldn't refuse. He suggested we meet up. I wouldn't have agreed, but then he said it was about getting even with Costello. But I never went along with any killings. I didn't know about those boys."

"But you knew he'd killed Emily?"

She nodded. "I was angry with him. He didn't have to do that. She was dead when I found her. What I told you about that is true. Even after all these years I recognised her. I couldn't believe what Trent had done."

"Didn't you try to stop him at that point?"

"I couldn't. He wouldn't listen. Trent said we'd bring him down. We'd make sure the police had enough on him to put him away. Once that happened, Trent planned to take over as much of Costello's empire as he could get his hands on."

"We understand why you would hate Costello," Imogen said. "But what did Trent have against him?"

"I don't know the whole story. Trent was cagey. But it has something to do with a robbery that all went wrong. It was planned by Costello and his people, but there was a leak. The police found out and set armed response on them. People were killed."

"Was Trent in on that robbery?"

"I don't think so. I'm not sure. He's very bitter about what happened.

"Why did you involve Kayne Archer and his mates?" Eliza King asked. "Archer was told to contact me specifically and tell me a load of lies."

"I have no idea. Trent didn't tell me everything. I didn't imagine for one second that he'd kill anyone. I've been a fool. I told him all about that night when my mother was killed, but he told me nothing. He never explained what he'd do with the information. Now I see that he used it to get to Emily."

"Why?"

"She took the gun off me that night. She must have kept it all these years. That gun was Costello's. Trent must believe it is significant."

Only if that could be proved, and Calladine doubted that. Even if it had been used to kill Mary Slater they didn't have a body. And with no body, no bullet. Even then they'd have their work cut out proving who shot her. Tanya had only been six and many years had passed. She was not a credible witness. So what was Trent's game?

Chapter 21

Tanya Mallon was taken back to the cells. The day was fast disappearing. They needed to find Trent before he vanished for good.

"Our plain clothes has been on from the Pennine Inn, sir," Rocco told Calladine. "Trent is still there. Word has it that he's been in a golf tournament all afternoon and it's about to finish."

"You and me. Eliza? Want in on this?"

"Absolutely. I want to give that creep a piece of my mind," she said, following them to the car. "He's given me the run-around for long enough. Though I can't for the life of me understand why."

"Neither can I, but we'll ask him."

"Trent talks Tanya into helping him frame Costello. That sorted, he sets about enrolling Archer to act as a go-between. Emily Blackwell is beaten and shot. Two of Archer's mates get it. But I'm still no nearer understanding what Trent is up to," she said.

"I think Trent wants to lure Costello into the open. Render him vulnerable. You know what his security is like," Calladine reminded her. "As a rule no one gets near.

But this situation has thrown him. Whoever has orchestrated this has gone for a two-pronged attack. A turf war blackens Costello's name. It ruins the years of work that have gone into making him appear legit. Then there's whatever the informant is supposed to know. That could be anything. Given that Emily Blackwell has been murdered, Costello must wonder if it has to do with Carol and Clough Cottage."

"Are you saying that Trent wants Costello dead?"

"Yes, I think he does."

"Does that mean Costello is in danger?"

"As ludicrous as that sounds — yes, I think he is."

"Where is Costello now?" Eliza King asked.

"On his way back to wherever he came from, if he's got any sense."

"So Trent has missed his opportunity?"

Calladine shrugged. "I'm not sure. What do you think Costello will do when he learns we plan to open that grave?"

"Even so, Trent is taking a chance. There is no guarantee that Costello would fall for the plan."

"Where Carol Rhodes is concerned, he doesn't think straight."

"Do you think Costello does want the Hobfield?" asked Rocco.

"No. Not for one second. But there's something else that has muddied the waters. People have been killed, allegedly on Costello's say so. If he didn't give the order, he will come looking for whoever did."

"Two ways he might be tempted into the open."

"Yes, Eliza. Someone is making dead sure that Costello gets within his sights."

Rocco drove them up the narrow country lanes to the Pennine Inn. He pulled into the small car park.

"You go have a word with the manager first, Rocco. Check on Trent's whereabouts. In the meantime we'll have a look around." He nodded to Eliza.

"Nice place," she said, casting her eyes over the old stonework. "I'd stay here myself if I had the money."

Calladine chuckled. "Expenses?"

"You're joking. The budget is so tight we might as well not have one."

They had a quick look into the dining room. It was empty. Then the pair of them walked towards the bar.

Rocco met them in the hallway. "He's disappeared, sir. The barman told me we're not the only ones looking for Trent." He nodded towards a seat by the window. "The plain clothes said it's all been very quiet. But he wouldn't recognise him, would he?"

"Costello! What's he doing here?"

"Probably the same as us, sir," Rocco whispered.

"I don't see any of his people."

"I think they must be his." Rocco nodded towards a couple of hefty-looking blokes standing by the entrance. "I passed them when I went to the manager's office."

"I don't want to approach Costello mob-handed. You two wander around. See what you can find out." Calladine left them and walked towards Costello. "On your own?"

"Not anymore I'm not," he barked. "Follow me up here, did you?"

"No. I thought you'd be well gone by now." Calladine sat down beside him. "Trent?"

Costello looked at him. "Thought I'd have a word. Seems the bastard is killing people in my name."

"Candid of you to tell me that, Mr Costello."

"Words, Inspector, just words. We're on our own. You can't prove a thing."

"Who is he, this Trent? And why is he doing this?"

"I haven't a clue. But when I get my hands on the bastard he'll rue the day, take my word for it."

"He's been causing a lot of trouble lately. He's killed people. The word is out that those deaths are down to you. He's told people you want the Hobfield and you'll get rid of anyone who stands in your way."

194

"I wouldn't waste my time. The place is a cesspit."

"That is what I told my colleagues. So then I got to thinking. What is it Trent really wants?"

Costello laughed. "Perhaps he intends to blackmail me."

"I think he intends to kill you."

* * *

"My name is Colin Barker, I'm a solicitor."

Tanya Mallon looked at the man. "I didn't ask for a solicitor."

He smiled. "It is usual in these circumstances. Do you want to ask me anything?"

"When can I get out of here?"

"I'm doing my best to get you bail."

"I can't spend the night here. I'll go insane. I've got none of my things and I need to eat."

"Actually you don't look very well. Let me get you a drink."

"Not more of that dreadful tea, please."

Barker held up what looked like a soft drink bottle to the uniformed officer stood by the door. "May I offer her some of this?" The officer nodded.

"Drink this. It has a drop of brandy in it," he whispered. "Put the colour back in your cheeks."

Tanya Mallon took a swig. It didn't occur to her that offering brandy was something a solicitor just wouldn't do. She was too tired. Anyway, the alcohol would lift her spirits.

"Do you have anyone who will stand bail for you?"

She shook her head. "Can't you pull some strings?" She took another swig of the drink. The alcohol hit the spot. He started rambling on, saying things she didn't understand. She wanted him to stop. She began to sweat. She hadn't eaten, and the brandy must have gone to her head. Tanya felt very weird. Suddenly there was a flurry of activity in the cell. She'd fallen to the floor in a faint.

Someone was shaking her arm. "Mrs Mallon? Wake up! You're not well."

She tried to answer but her voice wouldn't work. A male voice shouted, "Can you hear me? I'm a doctor. We are going to get you to the hospital."

Two policeman ran into the cell. Again she tried to speak but she couldn't. The cell was spinning. She screamed out as everything went black.

* * *

"Don't you have a home to go to?" Imogen asked Joyce.

"I'll sort through the last of this paperwork first. I don't mind, there's no one waiting for me."

Joyce didn't talk much about her private life but Imogen knew that she was divorced and lived alone. She felt sorry for her. Joyce threw her all into the job. There didn't seem to be much else in her life.

"Call for you," Joyce said, patching it through to Imogen's desk.

"It's Ricky Blackwell," Imogen mouthed back.

"I want to speak to that inspector," he told her.

"He won't be back for a while. Ricky? Are you with your aunt?"

"We're staying in a cottage in South Wales. It belongs to a friend. We want to come home," the lad said. "It was a mistake to run away. We can't afford it. But my auntie is scared."

"Did someone threaten her? Costello?"

"No, not him. That other bloke. The one who kept ringing my mum. We got a call after one of your detectives came round. He wanted to talk to Enid. He said he'd make sure auntie never spoke to anyone again. She was so terrified we took off."

"When are you coming back?"

"Tomorrow, but auntie won't come unless we're met at the station. The coach gets in at midday."

"I'll arrange it, don't worry. You and your aunt will be fine. Do you know who this man is?"

"No. Just that he offered my mum a lot of money if she got something for him."

"Do you know what?"

"No. She said I was better off not knowing."

"We'll look after you both, Ricky. You must come back and speak to us. Inspector Calladine won't let you down. Will you give me the address where you're staying?"

"I can't. Auntie said not to." With that he rang off.

"Joyce, get that call traced will you?"

Imogen went to the board. Tanya said Emily took the gun off her. Was it possible that she'd kept it all these years? Was that what Trent wanted?

"They say it'll take a while."

"I'll wait, Joyce. You get off home. It's been a long day."

The duty sergeant looked in. "The inspector here?" Imogen shook her head. "Tanya Mallon has been taken to hospital. She suddenly keeled over while she was talking to that solicitor of hers. She's been fine all afternoon. Complained of being fed up, but it wasn't anything to worry about."

"I'll get down there."

"What about the call you're having traced?" Joyce asked as she was putting on her coat.

"They'll leave a message. It's more important to see what's going on with Tanya. I'll ring Calladine with an update once I'm there."

Had they pushed Tanya too far? She might have come across as tough but Imogen had caught a glimpse of her softer side. She'd wept when she talked about her mother. Whatever happened all those years ago had left an emotional scar.

It only took five minutes to drive the short distance to Leesdon General. Imogen parked up and went into A&E.

When she arrived at Tanya's bedside two doctors were busy trying to resuscitate her.

"Do you know this woman?" one asked.

"Not personally. I'm police," she said, showing her badge. "Her name is Tanya Mallon. She's been in custody in one of our cells all afternoon."

"Did she take anything?"

"She will have had tea to drink, water perhaps." She checked her watch. "The food won't have been dished up yet."

"She's been poisoned. She either had something with her or she was given it."

"That's not possible. She'll have been thoroughly searched. I don't get it."

But Imogen could see for herself how serious Tanya's condition was. The monitors she was connected to were barely registering.

"Who brought her in?"

"A doctor was called to the cell. He called for an ambulance."

"What sort of poison has she taken?"

"We hoped one of you might be able to tell us."

Imogen looked at the uniformed officer standing in the doorway. He shook his head. "We found nothing."

"Did she have any visitors?"

"Her solicitor, that's all."

"Did she ask for one?"

"There's nothing logged."

Imogen felt sick. She knew what this was. Tanya Mallon had been got at. This was down to Trent or Costello. But how? She went outside and rang the nick. The duty sergeant answered. "Has any of Inspector Calladine's team returned yet?"

"No," he replied sharply. "That woman in custody. The one taken to hospital. Is she alright?"

"She isn't as it happens. Why do you ask?"

"Ten minutes after the ambulance left here another one turned up. Said there had been no mistake. They were here to take her in. Went away in a right strop. They had no idea what had gone wrong."

But Imogen had. Whoever had picked up Tanya Mallon and brought her to hospital was not from the ambulance service.

* * *

"Kill me! He wouldn't dare!" Costello bellowed. "Who is this creep?"

"We've no idea," Calladine replied. "We think he came here to lure you into the open. You need to be careful."

Costello laughed. "Worried about my safety, Inspector? He wouldn't dare." He took a mobile from his pocket and spoke into it. Seconds later two of his henchmen walked into the bar.

Costello grinned at them. "Apparently I'm in danger. Take another look around. See if you can find this man Trent. Check the rooms if you have to. The inspector will look after me until you get back." He patted Calladine's knee.

"This isn't a wind up," said Calladine. "Trent hasn't gone to all this trouble for nothing. He set those boys up. Recruited them for a rival firm then had them killed — by your people."

"*Allegedly* by my people. The truth is very different. I run a number of respectable companies. I do not have people killed."

"Well, not anymore," Calladine replied.

"Barman!" Costello shouted. "More drinks here. Want something, Inspector?"

"No thanks, I'm working."

Rocco and Eliza walked into the bar.

"This pair with you?" said Costello. "I know her. Anything goes down on the Yorkshire coast I'm the first person she drags in."

"I get the feeling she doesn't like you much."

"It's mutual. She's a mad bitch. I've told her, much more of her nonsense and I'll sue."

"The place is quiet, sir. Most of the rooms are empty." Eliza hung back, her arms folded. She didn't look at Costello.

The barman called across. "Whisky, sir?"

"Bring the bottle over, Robin."

"I'd feel happier if you were less visible."

"Sorry to disappoint, Inspector. I'm not in the habit of hiding in a corner. This scumbag wants me, he'll have to come out into the open."

Rocco was standing in front of the table looking through the window. He was nervous. This situation could become very dangerous at any moment. Costello was a volatile man. Rocco moved aside to allow the barman access. The barman was carrying a heavy tray. It held a bottle of single malt and a tea towel, under which Rocco presumed were glasses. But he let it slip. The tray landed on the table with crash and the bottle hit the floor. During the split second when everyone's attention was diverted, the barman snatched a revolver from under the tea towel.

"Stay put!" he ordered. "Don't even flinch." He pointed the weapon at Calladine, who was about to get to his feet.

"You are Trent?" Rocco asked.

"No. Tell them who I am, Costello." He held up his hand. Half of his little finger was missing.

"Robert Silver."

"But you've been calling yourself Trent."

"Yes, Inspector. Although we've never met, Silver is a name Costello knows too well." He jabbed the gun in Costello's chest. "Get up!"

"You can't hope to get out of here. His people are all over the building."

Silver looked at Calladine. "You don't get it, do you? This is about getting him. Getting even, not getting away." He shrugged. "If I do get out of this, it's just a bonus."

"What did Costello do to you?"

"He killed my son, Ryan. Shot his arms and legs to pieces then threw him in a lake and left him to drown."

"You should have come to us."

Silver snorted. "You lot are useless. Look at you now. You're drinking with the bastard. Ryan took part in that Cheshire job. Then this piece of shit thinks Ryan spilled his guts to the police so he punishes him. Made an example. That's what you called it, wasn't it Costello?"

Wearily, Costello got to his feet. "We'll take this outside."

Silver pushed him, the gun poking into his back. As he manoeuvred between the tables, Eliza King stuck out her foot. Calladine lunged forward, sending Silver face forward onto the floor. The gun jolted from his hand and slid across the carpet. But not before he'd fired it. Costello fell, blood pouring from his back.

Chapter 22

"What are you lot doing here?" DC Imogen Goode asked as the ambulance and police car pulled into the hospital car park.

"Costello's been shot," Rocco told her. "And we've arrested Silver — or Trent as we thought he was called."

"Well done!"

"It was down to DCI King really. She's a cool one alright. Silver was about to make off with Costello and she sticks out her foot, trips him up. Foolhardy, the boss said, but it worked. Silver has been working as a barman at the Pennine Inn for weeks. Called himself Robin. The same Robin who backed up Tanya's story. But for the purposes of getting Costello he set himself up as Trent. The only person who'd have known his true identity would have been Tanya Mallon."

"Where is the boss?"

"That car over there."

What she was about to tell him wouldn't make Calladine happy. "Sir, Tanya Mallon is dead."

His eyes shot up to meet hers. "How? When did this happen? She was locked up, for God's sake!"

"She was taken ill in the cells. An ambulance picked her up from the nick. But it can't have been genuine. By the time the real ambulance turned up she was gone. The doctors here think that something lethal was administered on the journey here. Doctor Bower is coming here straight away to do the post-mortem."

"She certainly wasn't blameless but she didn't deserve to die." He was furious. No Tanya, no more case against Costello. The chances had been slim before, but now they were non-existent.

"Oh, and Ricky Blackwell phoned. They are coming home tomorrow but want picking up at the coach station. They are terrified of some man who has been threatening them."

"Silver."

"Ricky didn't say. What have you done with Silver?"

"He's locked up at the station. He's virtually admitted he's behind the lot. Killing the lads and making out it was down to Costello. And the scam about having information. We'll talk to him later." He checked his watch. "It's getting late. We might leave it until tomorrow."

"And Costello? Is he badly hurt?"

"I'm just going in to find out."

* * *

Costello grinned at him. "They tell me I'll live, Inspector. Be sure to thank that bad-tempered bitch for me. I bet she can't believe what she did! Hates me, she does. She blames me for that stupid kid of hers being like she is."

Calladine didn't comment. Eliza had spoken only briefly about her daughters. "What's the damage?"

"Thankfully I'm a tad overweight." Costello pointed to the dressing at the side of his waist. "The bullet went through here. Straight through. Hit nothing but blubber."

"You were lucky."

"What will you do with Silver?"

"Charge him. After we've heard what he's got to say."

"His son was a muppet. He deserved everything he got."

"So you did know Ryan Silver?"

"Yes, but not like his father said. I wasn't responsible for any robbery. The lad worked on my security team. He had an accident. I can't see to everything. Things go wrong."

"I will have to talk to you again, Mr Costello."

Costello shouted to the hulk standing guard by the door. "Gregor! Give the inspector my card."

Calladine walked out into the evening sunshine. He doubted they would get anything to incriminate Costello. The Cheshire robbery had been thoroughly investigated at the time. "You might as well call it a day," he told the others, who were waiting in the car park. "Where's Eliza gone?"

"Back to the nick," Rocco replied. "DCI Birch has been on. Ken Blackwell was killed this afternoon in Strangeways. He was knifed in the showers."

Calladine groaned. He knew what this was. Costello was clearing up. Costello might or might not know that Tanya was Mary Slater's daughter but she was still a threat. Ken Blackwell had driven the van used to move Carol's body. Now there was no one left to tell the tale but Costello himself.

"What really gets me is that all this was done while he was quietly supping whisky in that bar."

His phone rang. It was Shez Mortimer.

"I'm waiting for you in the Wheatsheaf. I've been here ages. Where are you?"

"Case got complicated."

"You're the complicated one, Tom Calladine. I can't get near. Are you coming for a beer or what?"

He could do with speaking to her about Robert Silver. "I'll be with you very soon. Get me a pint in."

Imogen was looking at him. "Monika?"

"No, it's someone else," he admitted. "A woman I met the other day. She is loosely connected with the case. She might have some more information. So if anyone asks — it's work."

* * *

Ruth was getting at him behind his back again. From the way Imogen and Rocco had looked at each other, Calladine knew she had been talking to them.

The Wheatsheaf was busy. Three TV screens were blasting out a football match, and the patrons were noisy. Every time boot touched ball there was a storm of swearing or cheering. The quiet corner at the far end had been taken by three women and a horde of kids. A pushchair blocked the way to the table by the window where Shez was sitting, and spilt juice was all over the wooden floor making it slippery.

"This place gets worse," he grumbled to Shez, kissing her cheek.

She smiled. "I don't know. It's quite entertaining. Don't you like football?"

"I can take it or leave it," he said.

"I was beginning to think that's how you felt about me."

"The case got a bit heavy earlier. I couldn't get away."

"What are you doing this weekend?"

"A bit of R and R if I'm lucky." Then he remembered. "I've got a christening on Sunday. My sergeant, Ruth, is having her baby son done. I'm the godfather." He grinned.

"I was hoping we might go away somewhere."

Calladine's face dropped.

"What's the matter? I'm not that bad, surely?"

"I can't. Sunday's taken, and if I get Saturday free I'll spend it in bed."

"It's too soon, isn't it? I've always been a fast cow. I should learn how to control myself. Here we are, practically strangers, and I'm asking you away for the weekend."

Calladine put his arm around her. "It's not that. I liked you the instant we met. It's the job. It's always the job. But we'll have our little break together soon. Promise."

"Who's your plus-one for the christening?"

He pulled a face. "My mother."

She was looking at him expectantly. "You could take me. All you have to do is ask."

"Okay, why not? The do is in here afterwards. You can stay at mine on Saturday."

"Will I get to meet your friends?"

Panic gripped his stomach. Monika! He'd have to speak to her — and Ruth. Set them both straight. Monika was never going to work anyway. He changed the subject. "Robert Silver. What do you know about him?"

"Nothing much. He was a customer who at the first opportunity went off with the cheaper option. He came into the office to book someone to accompany him to a function and she stepped in — Annette. Thought she could set up on her own with my customers, cheeky mare!"

"Did you ever meet him?"

"Once or twice. He is friendly with some other customers on my books. I've told you this already," she reminded him. "Is it important?"

"Not anymore."

Chapter 23

Saturday

"Tell me about Tanya Mallon."

Robert Silver sat opposite Calladine and Rocco in the interview room, with his solicitor beside him.

"She had information I needed. My son worked for Costello. He found out about the girl, Carol. Costello talks about her a lot. Drives his wife wild." He sniggered. "After Ryan was killed I did a little research. Carol had had a friend — Emily Blackwell. I found Emily and leaned on her. She told me what had happened that night. She also told me about Mary's Slater's daughter. Some more research and I found Tanya. We were drawn together. We had something very powerful in common: a mutual hatred of Costello."

"Did you kill Emily?"

"She stopped being helpful. I gave her money but she clammed up. Emily Blackwell had Costello's gun. Even he didn't know that. He'd no idea what had happened to it. Emily kept it as a form of insurance."

"She gave you the gun?"

"I threatened to kill her son if she didn't."

"What did you do with Emily's things, her bag and phone?"

"Threw them in the canal."

"Why did Davey and Garrett have to die?"

"I needed to flush Costello out. I paid Archer to promise information to you lot. Stuff that would put Costello away." He laughed. "Don't we all wish that that bit was true! Archer thought he was working for one of Costello's rivals. Stupid fool didn't think it through. They had to die. Costello would get the blame and he'd be forced to show himself, clear his name." He went quiet. "You were supposed to go after him. Bring him in, charge him." He paused. "He's not paying you too, is he?"

"Your plan had merit, Silver," said Calladine. "Except for one big flaw. Costello is way beyond wanting anything to do with the Hobfield. He's not interested."

"But the plan worked. He did show himself, didn't he? He got worked up about something and made mistakes. If you hadn't blundered in when you did, he'd be dead now."

Calladine knew what that something was: Carol Rhodes. Emily's murder must have shaken him. He'd come to Leesdon for the police interview without demur. He'd wanted to assess the situation for himself.

* * *

"That's quite a confession, sir."

"He's got nothing to lose. Silver is a man consumed with grief after what happened to his son. He was willing to die in the process of getting his revenge. But he wasn't thinking right. The things he did — shooting Davey, beating and killing Emily. He went too far, but getting Costello overrode everything."

"Enid Mason and Ricky Blackwell are here, sir," Joyce told him. "And Professor Batho would like a word."

"Rocco, you and I will speak to them but I'll just ring Julian first."

"Tanya Mallon was given a massive dose of insulin, Tom, by injection. Sedated first then finished off."

"The ambulance that left her at the hospital. We've been unable to trace it, or the doctor that came to the cells. Both he and the solicitor must be in Costello's pay."

"Did the solicitor give a name?" Batho asked.

"Yes. He doesn't exist. Not as a solicitor anyway."

"The gun. There is a name etched on the barrel. It's badly worn and difficult to make out but it could say 'Vinny.'"

"Can we prove that?" asked Calladine.

"Doubtful. It looks as if someone's taken a grinder to it in an effort to obliterate the letters. To the teenage Costello it must have seemed like a good idea, scratching your name on a weapon. Whoever ground it clean did him a favour."

"Okay, thanks. If you get anything else, let me know."

Enid Mason and Ricky were drinking tea in the soft interview room. Enid looked ill.

"I've been terrified," she admitted. "The threats, and after what happened to Emily. We had to leave. I couldn't take much more."

"We've arrested the man who killed your sister," Calladine assured her. "It would have helped if you'd spoken to us earlier. You knew things. You knew about Jet Holdings and Costello, didn't you?"

She nodded. "It's never wise to talk about that man, Inspector. He has a wide reach."

"Did Emily speak to you about that night? We know she brought Tanya to your flat. You must have wondered about the child."

"Yes, she told me the whole story," Enid said. "We looked after Tanya for a day or two but we knew we couldn't keep her. I took her to the children's home in Oldston. I told them I'd found her wandering about

209

Clough Bottom on her own. The police investigated, I imagine. But they couldn't find Mary, so Tanya went into foster care."

"Did Emily ever say what happened to Mary Slater?"

"She was shot."

"What happened to her body?"

Enid stared out of the window for a few seconds. "It makes me go cold each time I think about it. And now someone else is living there. Supposing they find her?"

"Enid. Where is Mary Slater?"

"Vinny Costello threw her down that well of theirs."

* * *

"The well has been dry for years," Imogen told them. "The Nadens are having a new water system installed. I've been up there. The place is a mess."

"What will be left of her after all these years, sir?"

"Bones, Rocco, and not a lot else I would imagine."

"Julian is up there now with a team," Imogen said. "It might take a while. All sorts of rubbish has been thrown down there."

Eliza King came into the office. "I'm off now. It's been okay working with you lot. Just a shame about the outcome."

Calladine looked up from Ruth's desk. "Not getting Costello, you mean."

"That would have been the icing on the cake. Never mind. I'm sure I'll get another crack at him." She smiled at Calladine. "And thanks for putting me up."

DCI Birch entered the office. "Silver was a good call," she told the team. "You leaving us so soon, DCI King?"

"Yes. And it's DI King now that I'm no longer seconded to this station."

"Back to Yorkshire?"

"Via Daneside. DCI Greco is back and wants to brief the new team. That includes me, apparently, for a week or two."

"Best of luck with that." Calladine just couldn't begin to imagine it. The red-haired firebrand and the detail-obsessed Greco. What a combination!

"That grave, Calladine. I've got special permission for it to go ahead tonight," said Birch.

Tomorrow was the christening. Would they recover the remains and have it closed in time? The last thing he wanted was Ruth on his back for this too.

"I'll take a ride up to Clough Cottage. Imogen, want to come?"

"Not really. The place upsets me. We nearly bought it. If we had, I could never have lived there. I don't know how Annie Naden is going to manage."

"I'll come," Rocco piped up.

Calladine rolled his eyes at the others. "Morbid interest."

* * *

The fine weather had broken and there was a sharp wind blowing across the hill. "It'll rain before long," Calladine said, looking at the blackening sky.

Rocco was looking around him. "Weird place this. And now that we know what went on it's even worse."

"Nonsense. Done up, that cottage will be a great place to live."

"Julian's over there, sir." Rocco pointed.

The forensic scientist was rooting through a pile of debris. He was wearing a white coverall, and shrouded in dust and dirt.

"What have you got there?"

Julian Batho was moving an object around with a small trowel. "If I'm not mistaken, it's part of a human radius." He looked up. "One of the lower arm bones."

"So Mary Slater is down there?"

"It looks like it. But we'll have to do the DNA testing to make sure."

"We have nothing of hers to match it against."

211

"We have her daughter's DNA. That should give us the answer."

"Thanks, Julian. Do you know about the grave later on?"

He sighed. "I'll have a team standing by. Excavating the well is going to take some time, Tom. And it will be weeks before we have a definitive answer as to who this is. Who have you got in the frame?"

"It's down to Vinny Costello but we have no evidence. So the short answer is no one."

"And the rogue body in the grave?"

"Carol Rhodes, we suspect. But again — no evidence. This is a retrieval exercise, Julian."

Calladine and Rocco walked away towards the car. "Pity. Two women dead and we can't bring anyone to book."

"I know, Rocco. It gets to me too. But we got Silver. There's plenty of evidence to send him down for a long time."

"And Costello?"

"Walks, doesn't he? As always."

Chapter 24

Sunday

"I'm dreading this."

Eve Buckley was fixing Calladine's tie. "You'll be fine. The vicar will tell you what to say."

"It's not that. It's Shez."

"The woman upstairs? The one singing her head off?" Eve smirked. "I take it she's coming to the christening too?"

Calladine nodded. "I haven't told Ruth. She is still expecting me to partner Monika. She'll break my flaming neck for letting her down again."

"Are we going straight to the church?"

"And that's another thing. We had to have a grave opened. It was happening last night. I hope they've closed it, or covered it up, because Ruth will never forgive me if it's just sitting there for everyone to gawp at."

"Don't be silly. You won't be able to see a thing. It'll be cordoned off. Probably even closed already."

Calladine checked his mobile. Nothing. He was expecting a call or a text from Julian, telling him what they'd found.

"Will I do?"

Shez Mortimer was standing at the foot of stairs. She looked stunning. Calladine whistled. "Loving the dress."

"Not too short?"

He smiled. "You can carry it off. This is Eve, my mother."

Eve Buckley moved forward and held out her hand. "Pleased to meet you. Good that you can join us."

Calladine's phone bleeped. It was a text from Julian. The wording was brief and simple. They had found a body. About a foot under the coffin of Doris Ludford. The theory that Carol had been put in the open grave back in 1969 was confirmed. They'd also found a locket around her neck with her name engraved on it.

"Look at the time. We'd better get going."

"Taxi?" Shez asked.

"I thought we'd walk," Calladine responded. "It's only round the corner."

"Well, it had better not be far. Have you seen these heels?"

"What about the dog?" Eve asked, giving him a pat.

"He can't come. He'll be fine here."

Calladine ushered the two women out of the front door and locked up. They walked together in front of him, chatting away. They were so different but they seemed to get on fine. Eve might be one of the wealthiest women in Leesworth but she was no snob. Shez made no secret of what she did for a living. Neither was she concerned about people's opinions of the way she dressed. She had a loud laugh, liked a drink and wasn't shy about sharing her views. He liked her and so, it seemed, did his mother.

* * *

There were dozens of people milling about the churchyard, waiting to go in. Calladine nodded at Rocco and Imogen. Rhona Birch was chatting to his daughter Zoe and her partner, Jo. Everything seemed relaxed enough. And then he spotted Ruth.

Shez was holding onto one of his arms and Eve the other. Ruth's face was like thunder.

"You look great. Like the suit," Calladine tried.

"A word." She smiled at the two women and pulled him to one side. "What are you playing at? Monika will arrive any second."

"It won't work. Monika knows that too if she's honest with herself."

"I could bang your heads together. And who's *she*, your *escort* woman?"

"Don't be like that. She's fun. We get on. Eve seems to like her."

"Eve is just being polite."

Calladine tried to change the subject. "Did you hear about the case?"

"I can see that Doris Ludford's grave has been temporarily covered. Down to you, was it?"

"Carol Rhodes was down there. We were right. And it looks like Mary Slater is in the well up at Clough Cottage."

"Who's in the frame?"

"Costello. But there is no evidence. Everyone else connected to that night back in 1969 is dead."

"The two young men off the Hobfield?"

"We got someone for that."

"In that case, you got a result. Don't beat yourself up. The job is hard enough."

Calladine grinned. "I can hear Harry crying."

"He's on one again. Jake's been wheeling him around trying to get him off."

"Want me to have a go?"

"No, you'd better stay put. Monika's arrived."

Calladine turned around to look. Monika was getting out of a taxi. There was a man with her.

"Who's he?"

"I don't know but he's got his arm around her."

"She's dumped me!"

"Looks that way, Tom." Ruth giggled. "Your face is priceless, and it serves you right."

"You're not very nice to me at times, Ruth Bayliss."

"Do you blame me?"

"Can we get this over with? I'm a bag of nerves."

"Don't be stupid. It'll be over in no time."

"I've had a hard week," he said to her, as folk began to enter the church. "I had to interview Vinny Costello at one point. Nearly threw up before that one."

"If you like I'll do you a swap. You come and look after that grumpy little bundle next week and I'll do your job."

"Can't be that difficult. I'm something of a natural. You said so yourself. When are you coming back anyway?"

"Don't know that I am," she looked at him. "I might decide to be a full-time mum."

Calladine stood stock still. "Please don't frighten me like that. After the week I've had, I'm delicate."

"You are so easy to wind up, Tom Calladine."

The End

Thank you for reading this book. If you enjoyed it please leave feedback on Amazon, and if there is anything we missed or you have a question about then please get in touch. The author and publishing team appreciate your feedback and time reading this book.

Our email is jasper@joffebooks.com

www.joffebooks.com

ALSO BY HELEN DURRANT

CALLADINE & BAYLISS MYSTERIES
DEAD WRONG
DEAD SILENT
DEAD LIST
DEAD LOST
DEAD & BURIED

DI GRECO
DARK MURDER
DARK HOUSES